Drowning Creek

Drowning Creek

Peter Crittenden

Drowning Creek

by Peter Crittenden

Copyright © 2024 Peter Crittenden

ISBN 978-195690-4-406

Printed in the United States of America

Published by Blacksmith LLC
Fayetteville, North Carolina

www.BlacksmithPublishing.com

Direct inquiries and/or orders to the above web address.

All rights reserved. Except for use in review, no portion of this book may be reproduced in any form without the express written permission from the publisher.

While every precaution has been taken to ensure the reliability and accuracy of all data and contents, neither the author nor the publisher assumes any responsibility for the use or misuse of information contained in this book.

Contents

Prologue	1
I	7
II	16
III	26
IV	31
V	47
VI	60
VII	68
VIII	75
IX	82
X	92
XI	97
XII	120
XIII	131
XIV	144
XV	153
XVI	157
XVII	167
XVIII	181
XIX	189
XX	196
XXI	205
XXII	215
XXIII	220
XXIV	237
XXV	239
XXVI	246
Epilogue	256

For those who left, never to return . . . and for those who returned, never the same.

Prologue

The two men sat within the screened-in veranda enjoying cold beers, conversing in Spanish. As they spoke, they observed a curious activity in the waters of the canal, beyond the edge of the property's lawn. The ridged back scales of an alligator were visible as the enormous reptile broke surface, arched up and dove down. Large bluefish leapt up from the water into the air in front of where the alligator had been. Then the alligator would surface, and then go down again, and again the bluefish would break surface, fleeing the alligator.

"*Señor Caimán*, he is fishing for his lunch," one of the men said. A Latin American man of medium height and build, well dressed and well groomed, obviously not of the class that does hard physical work. He had a pencil thin moustache, and it was obvious he received regular manicures.

The second man, also a Latin, also of medium height and build, also well-dressed but with a hardness about him that spoke of a life spent doing hard work in the out-of-doors. "Yes," he agreed, "but look." He pointed to the timbers shoring up the sides of the canal, "*Señor Caimán*, he cannot come up here."

"Ha ha," the first man laughed his agreement. "Señor, allow me to explain how our banking system works. You have heard of the crypto currency, yes?"

"Yes, of course."

"This is how we manage our funds. Large amounts of cash have always been a monumental challenge in the business of

Drowning Creek

the cartels. You will recall how even the great Pablo Escobar, for all his multiple, multiple millions, in the end he died impoverished because he could not get his hands on his cash. And even those troves of cash to which his men could access were subject to the ravages of the elements, being eaten by rats, falling apart from the wet and humidity of the earth where they had buried it.

"But nowadays we have the crypto, and things are so much more manageable. We store our money in crypto, out in the cloud. We purchase goods and services, buy and sell our product, real estate, cars, trucks, food, clothing, everything one requires, through the Dark Web, with the crypto. It is so easy and convenient."

"Yes, of course," said the second man. "The crypto is so convenient. We can do our business right beneath the noses of the government and their secret policemen."

"There is only one problem."

"What is that?" asked the second man.

"Our criminal enterprises call for a certain degree of teamwork. Oh sure, we could be against each other, as in the drug wars of the old days, but that is so counterproductive! Why claw at each other like a basket full of crabs when there is more than enough money for each and every one of us, and anyway we have enough trouble as it is with the gringos?

"It is absolutely necessary that we cooperate at some level, and so we maintain a very special relationship among those of us at the very top levels of our various cartels, in order to effectively go about our business. And so, we have created a sort of combined crypto account. Cartel crypto! Not all of our fortunes, of course, but a significant amount of working capital to create escrow within a virtual bank all our own, where amounts of money can be transferred between our organizations with convenience, absolutely out of the eyes of the authorities."

"It is necessary that more than one individual can access the crypto account, of course, to manage things," the first man continued. "But therein lies the problem. How to manage access across the different parties?"

"Yes," replied the second man. "How do you do this?"

"Passwords are problematic. They can be forgotten, and if written down, lost, or even worse, stolen."

"What about the bio data?" the second man suggested. "Fingerprints? Retina scans?"

"Yes, but what if a person dies, or loses an eye or a finger? There are still limitations," the first man shrugged.

The first man then placed a strange looking cylindrical object on the coffee table before them. About nine inches long, perhaps two inches in diameter, of a polished steel-like alloy with symbols and lettering inscribed upon it. A sleeve of the same metal slid back to reveal a gray, crystalline display panel. A larger panel on the opposite side featured a vivid blue-green mineral, perhaps opal. It was ultra high-tech, almost futuristic.

The first man ran his fingers along the length of the object, pressing an unseen feature which clicked open a hatch to reveal the inner workings of the object.

Four geared wheels lay nestled within the cylinder, aligned along a narrow shaft. The first man placed a well-manicured finger beneath this shaft, and gently lifted the entire array out

Drowning Creek

of the cylinder. "Each of these geared wheels represents access to an individual account within our cartel crypto bank."

The second man stared long and hard at the cylinder, its panels and inscriptions, the vivid blues and greens of the mysterious mineral surface panel. "Do you mean to tell me that I am looking at millions and millions of dollars, in that little thing?"

"Billions," the first man said quietly. "Billions and billions. More money than the Zuckerberg, or Bill Gates, even."

"*Santa Madre de Dios*," whispered the second man.

"Ah, but Señor! It will not operate without the fifth wheel, belonging to whomever is to access their organization's account within the virtual bank." The smooth man then produced from his pocket another geared wheel. "This is your wheel, which allows you to access your portion of the bank." He placed the little geared wheel upon the shaft in line with the others. "And now," he said as he snapped the metallic cylinder closed and slid home the sleeve, "the device is now actuated. You may use it to unlock your account – in conjunction with the app on your laptop – in order to deposit into your account, and to move any monies into the other accounts for payments for goods and services. Nobody can use the device without their own fifth wheel. The fifth wheel is the key! You must keep it separate from the device, and in a secure place, of course, never to lose it."

"*Bueno*," replied the second man. "I will deposit into my account, as soon as I return to my offices. I did not bring my laptop with me here, of course."

"Of course," the first man said as he re-opened the device and withdrew the fifth wheel. He produced a silver chain, threaded the wheel onto it, and handed it over to the second man. "Keep this wheel on your person. Keep the device in a separate place, secure. Bring them only together under the strictest of security."

"*Si, claro,*" said the second man. "How much would you recommend I place within?"

"Señor, this is your business of course, but I recommend a significant amount, and to deposit a portion of every transaction you complete – it is an escrow account, *¿claro?* We are after all moving large amounts of product across our territories, goods and services, human beings even. Each cartel organization has hundreds of billions in crypto currency, within our virtual bank. Your Andean cartel has been in operation for decades, I am quite certain you know how much you need to deposit, to cover operational expenses."

"Very well then," said the second man, pocketing the device. "Thank you for including myself and my organization within your bank."

"*De nada,*" the first man replied. The two men sat back and enjoyed their beers. They turned their attention again to the alligator, which still plied the dark waters of the canal. The second man noticed something.

"The waters of the canal, they have now come up," he said, pointing to where the level of the water was now all the way up to the banks of the canal. "The tide is high. *Señor Caimán,* he may now come here."

"This is true," the first man said. "One must take care, walking outside, when the high tide is here."

As he said this, the first man's eyes suddenly went wide, his jaw dropped and blood erupted from his mouth. The second man looked up to see a figure entering the doorway across the room behind the veranda. A gun man! He drew his pistol and fired several fast shots towards the figure in the doorway, dropping him.

Another figure followed and crumpled beneath a barrage of nine-millimeter bullets. "*¡Pindejo!*" the second man yelled as he fired, "*¡Maricón!*" There were now two bodies across the doorway, and other gunmen cowering beyond the doorway, out of line of the withering fire. "YOU WILL NEVER CATCH ME!" he yelled as he retreated, not even pausing as he slapped another fifteen-round magazine into his pistol. "*I AM GATO! I AM GATO!*"

I

"Believe nothing what you hear, and only half of what you see." – Special Forces Truism

Leon would never forget her eyes. Ivy's green eyes looked like orbs of jade, set against her light brown skin, and framed by her dark brown hair.

Beyond the fact that she was absolutely beautiful, Leon would never forget Ivy's eyes because the last time he looked into them, she was six inches underwater and he was pulling her lifeless body from the ice cold waters of Drowning Creek.

* * *

Camp Mackall is a mosquito and tick infested flatland of pine trees and swamp, thirty miles west of Fort Bragg, where paratroopers and Green Berets have been training since 1942. In the summer Camp Mackall is always ten degrees hotter than anyplace else in the surrounding areas, and ten degrees colder in the winter. The summertime is almost six months long and it's as humid as hell - as much as one sweats, one never cools down - and in the winter that humidity drives the cold right into the bone. It doesn't snow very often, what it does is freeze over - ice storms. The place sucks. There's a saying about the weather out at Mackall: "This shit sucks. I love how much this shit sucks. Maybe if we're lucky, the rain will freeze and it will suck even more."

Drowning Creek

The name tag on his uniform read Leonard, so his teammates called him Leon and it stuck. Nobody but his mother called him by his first name, ever since he'd joined the Army, and that was a long time ago. Leon was an NCO – a noncommissioned officer, a non-com, a sergeant – in the US Army Special Forces, also known as the Green Berets, and he'd been doing this for a long time. If asked if he was burnt out, he'd say yeah, maybe. Disgruntled might be the word for it. Leon figured he'd stayed in too long - because of the Forever War - and now he was just biding his time, waiting to drop his retirement paperwork and move on to the next thing, whatever that would be. He really had no idea what he was going to do with the rest of his life. Most days he was happy just to wake up and realize he wasn't dead yet.

Until his retirement date rolled around, Leon was working at the Training Group out at Camp Mackall. A call had come in early in the morning. The minute he walked into the team hooch, the Captain looked up at him. "Some troops found a body."

"Yeah?" he said.

"Down by the survival training area. Drowning Creek."

"They don't call it Drowning Creek for nothing," Leon said, "But drunk fishermen usually wait until the weather's a bit warmer before they fall off the bridge into the creek."

"Get down there and see what we got. I'm calling CID." The Criminal Investigation Division.

Leon went down to the survival area, about a twenty minute walk from the main cantonment area. It was a cold morning, the sky overhead gray, overcast. The path was just wide enough to get a small truck through the pine trees, brown pine needles and sand underfoot but he chose to walk, to stretch his legs after the long drive out to Mackall. When he got there, three trainees were standing around with their hands in their pockets, their rucksacks and rifles off to the side. One of them pointed into the water. "Over there."

Leon could see what was obviously a body, just below the surface in the shallows.

"What happened? How did you guys find the body?"

The middle one spoke up. "We were doing land navigation training, Sergeant. We were looking for a way across the creek, when we saw the body. So we called in, told them where we were and what we found."

"When was this?"

"About forty minutes ago."

"Then you were lost. The sun just came up twenty minutes ago, and this creek is the southern edge of the nav box. Good thing you found the body, or you'd be in this creek up to your necks trying to get across to the other side. Trouble is, there is no way across – it's a mile wide swamp, and it's colder than a well digger's asshole." Leon was speaking from personal experience - at some point in the Special Forces Q Course, sooner or later they find a reason for the trainees to end up in this water. It sucks no matter what time of year, but it especially sucks in the wintertime.

Leon walked into the water towards the body. It was late November, the water was icy cold. Even though the water was only up to his waist, it was so cold his heart almost felt like it stopped. Leon recognized her immediately, even beneath the surface of the water. Totally nude, Ivy was beautiful - even in death - as beautiful as he had ever known her. She apparently hadn't been in there very long, and her face was frozen into a haunted look of fear. Very disconcerting.

"Come on," he said to the troops, "Let's get her out of here."

The soldiers shuffled forward, moved into the water to stand around Ivy. Leon bent down, put his arms under her back and the guys followed suit. "One, two, three," he said, and they lifted her up, carried her to the bank and laid her lifeless body on the pine needles.

"One of you guys give me a poncho, I want to cover her up." The guys looked uncomfortable and didn't respond. Leon guessed the kids hadn't seen a dead body before, and neither of them wanted their personal poncho to touch it. He looked at the closest guy, read his name tape. "Kozlow . . . what the fuck . . . Ski."

"Yes, Sergeant."

"Give me your fucking poncho."

The young soldier shook his head quickly, as if he was snapping out of a trance. He went to his rucksack, pulled his tightly folded poncho out of an outer pocket and handed it to Leon.

"Thanks. I'll give you one of mine when we get back to the compound."

Leon wanted to cover her up because it just didn't seem right to leave poor Ivy laying there, bare naked in the cold hard morning light.

"Now stick around," he told the troops. "CID are on their way and they'll want to get statements. Tell you what, so we don't waste any more of your time than we have to, sit down and start writing statements and then I'll cut you loose back to your training unit. You can go to the chow hall or whatever, and I'll let your cadre know where you've been." Leon didn't want to become the CID's go-to guy in their investigation, but this shit was already FUBAR - Fucked Up Beyond All Repair – and there was no way Leon could distance himself from it. He was the ranking man on site, and worse, he knew Ivy personally.

* * *

It didn't take the CID long to show up. Coming down the trail was his Captain with two men and a woman in civilian clothes with distinctive bulges on their hips beneath their coats. They introduced themselves, flashed their badges.

"Special Agent Smith."

"Special Agent Brown."

"Special Agent Johnson." They each handed Leon their cards.

"Right," Leon said. They looked young, wet behind the ears. "What are you guys, E-4's?"

That disarmed them. The Smith guy grinned sheepishly. "Uh, I'm an E-6. Brown is an E-4 . . ."

Johnson spoke up, "I'm a WO2." He said it '*Double-U Oh Two.*' Warrant Officer Two.

"Okay," Leon said. "Well, this is what we got." he indicated the body. "Some trainees found her. I got their statements." He handed over three pieces of lined notebook paper.

Johnson squatted down and pulled the poncho back. Leon looked at the two younger agents. The girl – Special Agent Brown – seemed to handle it but Smith's eyes got wide. Johnson pulled the poncho back a bit further. "Yeah," Leon said, "she's naked."

"Any ID on her?"

"No," Leon replied. "She's NAKED."

Johnson looked up at Leon, then looked around. "How long ago did your guys find the body?"

"About an hour and a half, or so," Leon answered. "The guys came across the body right about dawn."

"Damn," he said, "All these footprints have contaminated the site."

"This isn't where she fell in," Leon said. "Or was thrown in, or whatever."

"How do you know?"

"For one thing, she wasn't skinny dipping – wrong time of the year for it and nobody skinny dips around here, on post. This is swamp water, and the place is full of ticks and red bugs, besides. She fell in or she was thrown in. Judging by her eyes being open and the look on her face, it looks to me like she was killed. I'm not a forensic investigator but judging by the marks on her throat she was probably choked to death. Then somebody threw her body in the water, upstream from here. We can go up the creek and we'll see for sure where anybody came through the bushes. Most likely, somebody threw her off the bridge. Send your two, uh, agents, up to the bridge and have them control the site because up there is where you'll find any sign of a person pulling a body out of a car and carrying it to the railing."

"What makes you so sure of all this?"

"She floated downstream. Upstream is the bridge, makes the most sense. Come on."

Leon set off with the warrant officer following him up the banks of the creek, back far enough where they could study the undergrowth. "See?" he said, "Nobody came through here." Johnson nodded. Leon pointed up to the bridge – a simple concrete span about fifteen feet above them. The other two agents were up there already on either side of the bridge. "Hold up where you are," he hollered to the agents on the bridge. "Don't walk around up there, there's gonna be sign where a car stopped." Then Leon turned to the senior agent next to him. "We need to go up there and see what we can see. I bet you dollars to doughnuts there's a lot of fresh sign on the shoulder of the road, right up there in the middle of the bridge."

Up on the roadway, Leon walked to the middle of the bridge, then got down flat on his belly and looked at the sand and grit on the shoulder, right where he'd pointed, to the midway point of the bridge. "Look," he said, "There it is."

"I don't see anything," Johnson said.

"That's because you're standing up there, looking down at it. Get down here and look at it, on level with the ground. Ant's eye level."

Johnson looked at Leon like he was crazy, but then he shrugged and got down on his belly next to him. Squinting and looking sideways, he said, "I'll be damned."

Drowning Creek

The tiny pieces of grit and sand looked fluffed up, obviously freshly disturbed. There were fresh scuff marks, prints in the gray grit almost an eighth of an inch deep, and drag marks. It appeared obvious that this was where somebody had gotten out of a car and dragged something heavy to the railing overlooking the creek. "You can read it like a book," Johnson said.

"Exactly," Leon said.

"But why would somebody throw her in the creek, knowing the body is going to be found after it floats downstream?"

"I dunno. People do stupid things. But I bet if you looked down there on the bottom of the creek, right down there," Leon pointed to where the body would have gone if a person heaved it over the railing, "You'll find a sheet or a blanket of a tarp or a poncho liner that was wrapped around her and weighted down, that came off and she floated away."

"Okay," he said, "We'll look into that. But even still, what does that tell us? How the hell we gonna figure out who came by here and threw her in the creek?"

"Well, I guess you could start by asking her husband."

"What do you mean her husband? You know who she is?"

"Yes."

"You DO?"

"Yes. Her name is Ivy Haglin. Maiden name Ivy Torres. I've known her for about ten years. Her husband is an officer in Third Special Forces Group."

"You're going to have to come down to headquarters. We're going to want to have a talk with you on this."

"That's what I was afraid of," Leon said. "Can I go get my bag from the team hooch?"

"Sure."

"Can I get some chow at the mess hall before I show up?"

"Sure. Of course. You know where our headquarters is?"

"Yes, unfortunately."

"Can you make it there this afternoon?"

"Sooner is better for me, actually. I got something to do here at 1500, so I'm going to have to be out of there and driving back to Mackall no later than 1400."

"That'll work," Johnson said. "I'll see you when I see you."

II

Leon pulled his truck into the parking lot at CID Headquarters down on Randolph Street, in a cluster of higher headquarters units. It was a part of Fort Bragg he usually avoided like the plague – the place was totally infested with REMFs – Rear Echelon Motherfuckers. The sooner he got this over and done with and got the hell out of 'Leg Land', the better.

He walked across the parking lot and into the foyer and stood in front of the bulletproof glass with the little round speaker in the middle of it. Behind the glass, a young soldier in uniform looked up. "Yes, Sergeant, how can I help you?"

"I'm here to see Special Agent Johnson."

"Is he expecting you?"

"Yes."

"Good, I'll let him know. Please take a seat."

Leon grimaced inside - the motherfuckers were going to make him wait. And wait. And wait. Leon knew what they were doing, *'The ol' Hurry-Up-and-Wait routine,'* he thought. It was their procedure to make a potential suspect sit there and sweat it out, stew in his own juices. *'Whatever,'* he thought, with a mental shrug.

Forty minutes later – right on cue - the private from behind the bulletproof glass finally came to the door. "Special Agent Johnson will see you now." Leon got up and she walked him back to a dimly lit office with a desk lamp. '*How cliché,*' Leon thought, '*Like something out of a movie.*'

Johnson and another guy came in and sat down at the desk. The other guy sat across from Leon, Johnson was at his three o'clock.

"Let's start with what we know," Johnson said. "When did you find the woman's body in the creek?"

"I didn't find her," Leon said. "Those trainees found her. I gave you their names and statements. Did you question them?"

"We got their names."

"Well, I'd like to ask you to do it right, guys," Leon said. "Don't pull them out of training to come down here and tell you they don't know the answer to a bunch of questions. If they lose too much time out of training, they'll have to recycle, and that's a major league aw shit."

"Are you telling us not to interview them?"

"No - don't put words in my mouth," Leon snarled. "I'm saying do the guys a common courtesy - go out to Camp Mackall and interview them there, so they don't lose too much time out of training. The Q Course is enough of a bitch as it is, it's even worse if you lose class time and fall behind. Besides, they don't know anything. All they know is they found a body in the Drowning Creek."

"Okay. What do you know? You knew the deceased?"

"Yes."

"How do you know her?"

Drowning Creek

"Half of Third Special Forces Group knew her. She was pretty much an SF groupie."

The recruiting literature says *'Special Forces is a Special Kind of Soldier'*. Well, a Special Forces Groupie is a special kind of woman. It's more than being enamored with the mystique and simply dating one of the guys. An SF groupie dates ALL of the guys, or as many as she can get her hands on. Some SF Groupies are quite adventurous, they date several Green Berets at the same time. That is, at exactly the same time and place.

"How long have you known her?"

"About ten years."

"SF groupie, huh? Were you ever with her?"

"No, but I know some of the guys who were."

"Any of them have any reason to kill her?"

"Let's see here – one of them is retired, living down in Atlanta - Jim was a good guy, everybody got along with him, can't see any angst between the two of them. Scotty is dead, last I heard, so I'm guessin' that kind of scratches him off the list. Then there's Haglin."

"Who's Haglin?"

"Rudy Haglin is her husband. You get in contact with him yet?"

"Of course not. Not yet. We didn't even know who the girl was until you told us, how would we know who to reach out to?"

"Good, then don't contact him. At least not right away."

"Why not?" Johnson asked.

"Think about it," Leon replied. "If you play you cards right, you've got your man."

"What do you mean?"

"Jeez," Leon said, "I gotta spell it out for you? Look, if you just rock up and flash your badge and say, 'Hey, Colonel, we just fished your wife's body out of the creek,' then that's it - he starts crying and moaning and it doesn't matter if he's guilty as sin, you've sold the farm and now he lawyers up and you have an uphill battle from there. How the hell did you even identify the body? There wasn't any ID on her, nothing, she was bare ass naked."

Leon continued, "But if you play it right, like, ask him - 'So hey, Haglin, where's your wife these days?' And he comes back with, 'Oh, she's visiting her mother,' or some shit like that, you know you've got him. Just let him keep talking long enough to dig himself deep into his lie, and then wham, you spring it on him like Colombo: 'Well, you know we just pulled her out of the creek this morning.' Then you watch his reaction and either he outright confesses or he backpedals, either way you've got him. Then you look inside his car, see if you can pick up any forensic evidence – Ivy's DNA in the trunk, dirt particles from the side of the bridge, anything – and you've got him lock, stock and barrel."

"Anyway, that's how I'd do it if I was you guys," Leon concluded. "But what do I know? I'm just a knuckle-dragging Neanderthal, hiding behind a rucksack."

"Okay," Johnson said. "We'll get back to that. What about you? What were you doing last night between the hours of, say, 2100 to 0400 in the morning?"

Drowning Creek

Leon looked at the guys, deadpan. "You've got to be kidding me – you think I did it? Explain to me, if I'd done it, then why would I have led you upstream to the bridge, showed you the boot prints and the scuff marks on the shoulder? That doesn't make much sense, does it?"

"I don't know if you did it or not, but you do seem to know the deceased pretty well, so that puts you within a pool of likely suspects. We have to cover all our bases."

"Yeah, I figured," Leon replied. "Well, for me this morning out at the creek was a great follow-on to last night, because last night I was downtown at the Cumberland County Sheriff's Department damn near all night."

"What was going on?"

"One of my troopies got his ass rolled up at a strip club down on Bragg Boulevard. Snarky's – you probably know the place, everyone does. There was some trouble with a bouncer at the door, he was drunk and they didn't want to let him in. When they rolled him a switchblade knife and a vial of coke appeared on the sidewalk, and then a Sheriff's deputy picked him up. They called me – Sheriff's deputy is an old teammate of mine from Group – so I went downtown to pick my guy up."

"They just handed him over to you? What about the drugs?"

"My buddy the deputy told me the bouncers have planted coke on G.I.'s before. It isn't even quality blow – they'll get just enough to get a reaction when the cops test it in the lab, step on it with baby formula and baking soda so there's over five grams - trafficking. He said the bouncers at those clubs are known to do that to permanently get rid of troublemakers. Deputy figured he was doing me a favor, saving me a shitload of paperwork by just handing the kid over to me."

"Seems like a pretty good deal."

"I told my buddy I wished he'd booked the kid," Leon said.

"Why?"

"This kid's a piece of shit, we've been trying to find a way to get rid of his ass. A bust like this would've been his one-way ticket back to Civvie Street."

"Hmmm. So, you've got an alibi."

"Iron tight. It was three in the morning or thereabouts by the time I got the kid signed back into the barracks," Leon went on. "Because of the law enforcement aspect to it, I had the C.Q. log the whole thing - I wanted to put the kid on the permanent shit list. Kid's doing a piss test this morning, just to see if the coke was his, or if, like the deputy said, the bouncers planted it on him. Which I don't necessarily believe, by the way."

"Why not?" The other agent spoke up.

"Doesn't make sense," Leon answered. "If the kid was just showing up at the club, hadn't gotten in yet - only trouble was at the door - then why would the bouncers want to bounce his ass permanently when they could just kick his ass to the curb and say, come back later when you're not shitfaced."

"I guess so."

"Anyway, what the kid's story is the coke was planted on him by a stripper at another club he'd just come from, before he got to Snarky's."

"What?"

Drowning Creek

"I know," Leon said. "What a story, right? Bouncers roll the kid and find drugs on him, call the cops. Cop figures the bouncers planted the shit, calls me up to come get my guy, thinks he's doing me a favor. Kid doesn't even think to fall back on the story that the bouncers planted the shit on him, instead he tells me some fairy tale about a stripper planting drugs on him. So I knew right away he's full of shit – what stripper is going to part with her nose candy, right? The kid's a shitbag, the coke is his, the piss test is going to prove it and we'll be rid of his ass once and for all. The only aw shit about the whole thing is instead of kicking him out of the Army, we'll only be able to kick his ass over to the 82d Airborne, and they'll have to put up with his ass. I hate burdening the 82d with our ash and trash."

"Why can't you chapter him out of the Army on a piss test?"

"It's a training unit, he gets a training Article 15," Leon remarked. "A training Article doesn't follow a guy to his regular unit."

"Maybe he'll shape up," Agent Johnson offered.

"Maybe, but I doubt it," Leon replied. "If he can't stay straight and be wired tight when he's in the Q Course, how do you think he's going to be when he's down there trooping the line? Plenty of room for him to fuck up in the Infantry."

"We'll check out your alibi, of course, but you're basically in the clear."

"Thank you."

"You've had a long night, by the way."

"Tell me about it."

Johnson kicked back from the desk. "Would you like a cup of coffee?"

"That'd be nice."

Johnson looked at his sidekick. Sidekick stood up, "How do you take it?"

"Hot and black. Same way I like my strippers."

"Ha, ha." Sidekick went out of the room. Johnson looked at Leon.

"Like you said, if we just go straight to Haglin and tell him his wife's down in the morgue, he's going to put his guard up. So how do you suggest we spring this thing on Haglin?"

"Have you guys dragged the creek bottom yet? Down by the bridge?"

"No, why should we do that? We've got the body."

"You might find whatever he wrapped her in, maybe tried to weigh her down with. You'll probably find a poncho liner with his name written on it. Haglin is a nice guy and normally sharp as a tack, but people get stupid when they do something seriously criminal. Especially if the crime is murder."

"We'll have to go back down there. You can show us where," Johnson said.

"Fuck that shit."

"What are you talking about?"

"I ain't getting in that creek again. It's fucking late November, that water gets deep down by the bridge and its damn cold. I know – I've crossed that creek in the wintertime. Have your people do it, it's their job."

Drowning Creek

"Let's move on."

"Let's," Leon agreed.

"So how would you work this thing, with Haglin?"

"Very carefully, obviously."

"Obviously."

"It's gotta be someone who knows Haglin well enough to ask, 'how's Ivy these days?' and not make it sound fake."

"Any suggestions?"

"Sheesh, I gotta do everything for everybody all the time in this damn Army." Leon rolled his eyes. "Okay, how about this: you go to Haglin's commander, swear him to silence on a stack of bibles, read him the riot act, have him sign a non-disclosure statement as a member of the investigation or whatever it is you guys do when you plant one of your people into a unit, under cover. Then you have the commander tell Haglin – and all the rest of the staff officers - that they're having a wives meeting, the woman's auxiliary or whatever, in advance of an upcoming deployment, and as he's the operations officer in the organization, Ivy's participation is especially sought after, so could she show up Wednesday morning in the Battalion auditorium to help kick this thing off? That oughta do it."

"It's that simple?" Johnson asked.

"It's the best I got, what do you got?" Leon shot back. "I don't think inviting him to bring his wife around to a mandatory fun cookout is going to work, in late November."

Johnson shrugged. "I guess so. So we have the commander make up this thing about a spousal support group, then hope

Haglin makes up some bullshit excuse as to why Ivy can't show up."

"That's right. Whatever he comes back with is going to be a known lie. Then all you have to do is read him his rights and slap the cuffs on."

"How do you feel all about this?"

"Totally indifferent," Leon said, looking Johnson straight in the eyes.

"How so? You knew Ivy."

"Ivy was no friend of mine."

"Why? How so?"

"Long story. Where's that coffee?"

III

When Johnson returned with two cups of coffee, Leon said, "I guess I should tell you that story. Never know how it might help with your investigation."

"I appreciate that," Johnson said, blowing on his coffee. "Do tell."

"It's not a pleasant memory," Leon began. "It was about seven years back. There was this one guy, Steven Meisinger. We weren't on the same team but we'd been on a few deployments together and we got along as friends. He was a medic, one of the smarter guys, picked up languages pretty well and played a mean game of chess. I never really understood why the guys on his team didn't care for him, why he always hung out with guys on other teams. That is, until I got him on my team. After that I learned a lot more about Steve than I ever wanted to know."

Leon took a sip of his coffee. "It was in the Philippines. We'd just arrived in-country. The plan was to stay in Manilla for a couple days, acclimatize, get fully briefed at the embassy and get over our jetlag before we headed out to the provinces. Some partying was in order, of course. Turns out Steve was a total sexual deviant, and when we all headed out for the evening, Steve went his own way.

"Next morning at the hotel, I get a call to come downstairs. The Company Commander and the Sergeant Major were both waiting for me - there was a problem and it involved Steve. An older Filipina woman was there, a mama-san type, and she had a younger woman with her – one of her bar girls. Mama-san was royally pissed off, and the bar girl was in tears. Steve had taken the girl back to his room, and I don't know what he did exactly but apparently he'd destroyed her somehow and now Mama-san wanted payment because Bar Girlie was out of commission.

"The Sergeant Major growled at me: 'This is your problem. Steve is your guy. Deal with it.' Not the best conversation to have with the Sergeant Major at the beginning of a deployment.

"The entire episode was totally embarrassing and not the sort of thing anyone wants to deal with before their morning coffee. To make her go away I had to pay off Mama-san for what Bar Girlie would normally earn over the course of six weeks. Mama-san wanted three months' pay for the girl but I bargained it down to half. Steve was on my shit list after that and I had to keep him on a short leash. If the guys went out partying, Steve had to stay back and keep an eye on the gear. Any shit detail that came up, Steve's name was all over it. I'll say this in Steve's favor - he paid me off promptly, at least.

"About a year later – back here in the States – I came into work on a Saturday morning to get things together for an upcoming deployment and there in the team room was Steve, with Ivy. He was prepping his medical gear and for some reason Ivy was in there, hanging around. I already knew who Ivy was, of course – she was infamous throughout Group – and now she was with Steve. Interesting. I wondered if she'd gotten the Filipina Bar Girl treatment yet, or anything close."

Leon went on. "Meanwhile, ever since the Philippines thing, Steve had been steadily degenerating. The way he treated the

Filipina bar girl was just an indicator of an overall decline of mental stability. He got caught masturbating openly in his car in the mall parking lot in the middle of the day, goofy stuff like that. Like I said, I was learning a lot more about Steve than I cared to know. Lord knows what the hell Ivy was doing with him. Or should I say, what Steve was doing to Ivy, because what she eventually did to him was the single most insane thing I've ever seen a woman do to a man.

"Steve's psychosis had gotten to the point where he was losing contact with reality. His speech was becoming more and more disorganized, like a stream of consciousness fueled by hallucinations or delusions. I'm not a shrink, of course, but it wouldn't have surprised me if the shrinks told us Steve was a full-blown schizophrenic. We finally got the C.O. to sign the papers to send Steve to the psych ward for a 72-hour observation. Because he was my guy, I had to drop by to check in on him.

"So I'm at the hospital, heading up to the fourth floor. You know, the psyche ward," Leon continued. "The elevator door opens, I step out and the first thing I see is Ivy walking right towards me. She was in one hell of a hurry - walked right past me without saying a word, no eye contact, nothing – it was like I wasn't even there. She actually knocked me out of the way as she brushed past me, body-checked me like a frikkin' hockey player. I turned and watched her taking the stairs as she bolted out of there. Then I went into Steve's room."

Leon paused to take a sip of coffee. "Steve was collapsed back on his pillows, his throat was slit from ear to ear and blood was spurting out from his jugular."

"Jeez," Johnson exclaimed.

"Yeah," Leon acknowledged, pausing to take a swig of coffee. "Blood was spurting out all across the room. There was blood everywhere, blood all over the place. I jumped over to Steve and jammed my fingers into the wound in his throat to stop where the blood was spurting, and then looked around for some way of summoning some help, some kind of panic button. The phone was out of reach but there was a button on a cord next to the pillow so I reached over Steve with my free hand and mashed it."

Leon took another sip of coffee. This wasn't the kind of story that rolls out easily. "It seemed to take forever for the nurse to show. Meanwhile my fingers were all up into Steve's neck. I'd stopped the bleeding and he seemed to be breathing – his trachea hadn't been cut. It took even longer for the surgical crew to show up but when they did those guys were amazing, pure artists of their trade. They saved Steve's life."

Leon gestured with his hands. "So, I'm guessing the whole time I was staunching the bleeding there wasn't much oxygen getting to his brain because when it all was over, the docs told me they estimated Steve had had at least thirty mini-strokes from the time he'd had his throat slit until the surgeons restored the blood flow to his brain. Steve was done. *Non compos mentis*, a total basket case. His parents had to come out from Iowa to pick him up and take him home. It was sad. Steve was a total freak and a weirdo, and I guess he hurt some people, but that was a hell of a price to pay.

"There was an investigation of course and I had to talk to CID – you guys - and answer a bunch of very uncomfortable questions. I told them about how I'd encountered Ivy in the hospital corridor just before I stepped into the room and found Steve all messed up. To this day I don't know what Steve did to her, but apparently it was enough for Ivy to do what she did to him, and she somehow talked her way out of it, I guess."

Leon shifted in his seat. "I saw Ivy a few times after that but I never had a word to say to her. The nicest thing I could say about Ivy is that she was one scary bitch. She was still an institution around Group, ever the ultimate SF Groupie, SF Team Queen. Other guys would go with her, but I never had anything to do with her. I avoided Ivy like the fucking plague.

"I saw Ivy about a year after all that shit, on base at the Green Beret Club. She was at the bar with a pair of warrant officers. The warrants were in their Class As, and the three of them were all goofing around, the guys were sort of like 'sandwiching' her between them. Made me want to fucking puke. Then about a year or so later, Ivy actually got married – to Haglin, my old team leader of all people - who was by then a major and my Company Commander. She'd finally graduated from Team Queen all the way up to the C.O.'s Wife. Hard work and dedication pays off, I guess."

IV

It had been a long night and a longer day already, Leon was exhausted. Before he drove back out to Camp Mackall to check in and update the team on what they needed to know about the body, he needed to drop by headquarters and brief the First Sergeant on the dirtbag he'd dragged home from downtown, earlier that morning.

Leon had served in Special Forces a long time. As the saying goes, he'd "been there, done that, got the t-shirt." If one was to ask him to describe his time in the Army, like so many of his colleagues he'd say, "I've been to Bumfuck, Egypt, I've been up the creek without a paddle, and I've been there when the excrement hit the rotating ventilator." At this stage in his career, Leon was seeing out his last year in the Army riding herd on the trainees at Training Group. His job was to keep them focused and out of trouble while they went through the Special Forces Qualification Course – the 'Q Course'.

The Q Course is over a year long, and it's not all field training – there are days and weeks spent waiting in garrison for a class to start, and there is a months-long academic phase in the middle of the Q which is also conducted in a garrison environment - plenty of time for young troops to get into all kinds of trouble if you let them get bored. Leon actually enjoyed the opportunity to mentor the next generation of Green Berets. He enjoyed showing them tricks of the trade and answering their questions about life in the active Special Forces Groups.

Drowning Creek

There are five active Special Forces Groups, oriented to different regions around the world – East Asia and the Pacific, Africa, Central and South America and the Caribbean, and Europe. There is some geographical overlap between the Groups regarding their Areas of Operational Responsibility (AORs) but basically Special Forces soldiers study the languages of the regions their unit is focused on, and have ample opportunity to practice their language skills when they're 'in country', which is about six months out of a year. Special Forces missions include training and advising foreign armies, humanitarian missions such as response to natural disasters and evacuations due to political unrest, counterterrorism, counter narcotics missions and other 'Operations Other Than War', and of course working with indigenous forces during combat operations.

Special Forces soldiers are not shock troops such as Rangers or paratroopers - although there is a great deal of overlap in their missions and capabilities. Special Forces units sometimes task organize as assault forces for direct action missions, such as counterterrorism, although typically Special Forces operate in much smaller units with minimal logistical support. When the news media reports that the U.S. is sending 'military advisors' into some country – even in peacetime - those advisors are Special Forces soldiers. Green Berets also work out of embassies and other overseas locations where their language abilities and technical skills are suitable for various roles.

Over the course of twenty years Leon had served in the Middle East, East Asia and across the Pacific, Eastern Europe, Africa and Central and South America. He spoke four languages, had served as a military advisor to indigenous forces, had done counterterrorism work and humanitarian missions. He'd even worked out of embassies doing the 'Sneaky Pete' stuff, out of uniform and unarmed a good deal of that time.

Now, after all that hero stuff, Leon was basically just cooling his heels, working with the next generation and looking at retirement, waiting for the second part of his life to begin. But the Gods of Chance and Karma never sleep, and right on cue Ivy shows up dead in the middle of the swamps of Camp Mackall. So now Leon wasn't just a crusty old burnout, Leon was a crusty old burnout in the middle of what was shaping up to be a fine little shitstorm.

* * *

Ivy's body wasn't the first body to show up out at Camp Mackall during Leon's hitch, she wasn't even the first body he'd seen pulled out of Drowning Creek. Things happen, but the Army keeps rolling along. There were soldiers to train and Leon's job was to train them. That afternoon at 1400, one of the training teams was scheduled to present a brief back on their planned mission.

The brief back is a formal process where a Special Forces team, prior to inserting into an 'A.O.' - Area of Operations - briefs the commander on their upcoming mission. The intent is to ensure that the team understands every aspect of their mission, the overall objective of the mission, and their commander's intent. The brief back also ensures that the commander has confidence in the team to conduct the mission, and that the commander's staff understands the team's mission – where they were going, what they were doing, and whatever support they might require such as resupply drops or recovery, which could involve a helicopter coming in to pick them up, or a link up with regular forces.

Drowning Creek

The team was already in the room, seated along the wall, the team leader was standing in front of a large map with overlays depicting the enemy situation on the ground and phases of their mission. Leon recognized two of the soldiers - they were the two trainees who had fished Ivy from the creek, earlier that day.

The Training Group Commander walked in – a full colonel - the room was called to attention, military formalities and introductions attended to, and the briefing got underway.

The captain who was leading the training team – also a trainee – indicated on the map where the team was to infil by helicopter, where they expected to link up with 'guerrilla forces', potential enemy activities the team would observe and report, and be prepared to possibly attack, in concert with the 'guerrillas'. For the purposes of this training event, the guerrillas would be played by local civilians familiar with the training scenario and led by training group instructors, also playing guerrillas.

The team captain was followed by the team's intelligence sergeant who briefed disposition of enemy forces within the team's A.O., the friendly forces situation – in this case the guerrillas – and possible enemy courses of action - worst case, and most likely case. The team's communications sergeant briefed when they would make scheduled shortwave radio transmissions back to base and presented the classified instructions and code books – tucked into a cargo pocket on his trousers and secured by a piece of parachute cord – that included frequencies to be used.

The team's captain returned to the map and briefed when and where they expected resupply drops and helicopter landing zones for possible pick up and extraction. Finally, the team's intelligence sergeant returned to brief the outlines of their 'evasion corridor' – where they were expected to go if the tactical situation on the ground were to go against them and they required an emergency extraction.

The training team's captain concluded the brief, the Training Group commander gave his approval to the team to conduct their mission, and the team secured their rucksacks and rifles and moved out to the truck that would take them to the nearby airfield to get on the helicopters for infil.

When the team got to the airfield, however, there weren't any helicopters. Instead, there was only a very small twin-engine cargo plane – a short take-off and landing plane (STOL) - with civilian markings, parked on the tarmac. The students were not accustomed to seeing civilian aircraft out here at Mackall, only military helicopters and cargo planes such as the huge C-130s and C-17s which they used for their parachute training. The team captain looked at Leon, confused.

"There's been a slight change of plan," Leon explained. "Because of the tempo of operations in the conflict, all regular military air assets have been diverted for use elsewhere. But we have fortunately managed to get our hands on this aircraft, from another government agency."

"But this is not a helicopter," the team captain exclaimed. "It can't land to put us in."

"That's not going to be a problem," Leon replied. "See those parachute wings on your chest? This is where you earn your jump pay." He pointed to the packing shed next to the airfield. The lights were on, and through the windows the team could see support soldiers moving about, and parachute packs lined up on benches.

"A night jump?" the captain asked. "What drop zone? Where?"

"Come on inside, I'll brief you on the changes," Leon said. This was all a part of the scripted training scenario that the students did not see. The intent was to throw them off balance, to replicate the chaos and confusion of actual combat operations, where no plan survives contact and the only constant is change.

There was a map on the wall inside the packing shed. Leon briefed the team. "We will jump in here," he pointed to the clearing west of Camp Mackall, where the team originally planned to insert by helo. He pointed out the track of the aircraft – south to north – the jump altitude – 1250 feet, the north end of the drop zone where they would assemble after landing, and from there the mission would be as the team themselves had briefed it that afternoon. "I'm the jumpmaster," Leon said, "we have assets on the ground who will mark the drop zone with six lights, configured as an arrow, pointing north. The drop zone will only be lit for two minutes prior to our drop time, and two minutes after. I'll be jumping in with you to accompany you on the ground." This last seemed to reassure the trainees. "We're jumping combat equipment of course – rucksacks, rifles, everything. The whole nine yards."

This should have been a hint to the trainees the change in plan from helicopter infil to parachute jump was scripted into the training exercise all along. "Let's rig up," Leon said, "daylight's burning."

This last was a bit of dry Army humor, of course, because it was already dark, and there was no moon.

There's a saying: "The Army could ruin a wet dream." Anything fun in the sporting life, the Army will ruin it for you. Military airborne operations are nothing like sport freefall parachuting.

Burdened by parachutes, reserve parachutes, rucksacks and the weight of weapons, ammunition, water, radios and whatever other special equipment the mission requires – as much as a hundred and eighty pounds total, including their chutes – the troops waddled across the tarmac and loaded the plane via the cargo ramp.

The light cargo plane was nothing like a civilian airliner. The soldiers collapsed onto metal framed nylon cloth benches that line the inside walls of the aircraft, folded their hands over the reserve parachutes on their chests, and a crewmember seat belted them in because they were so overburdened by gear that they couldn't reach around to seat belt themselves. Small talk was impossible over the loud drone of the engines. The plane rolled towards the runway, came to a halt, and then the sound of the engines got louder as the rpm's ramped up. Then the pilot released the brakes, the plane rolled down the runway, picked up speed and lifted off.

Blacked out for tactical purposes, the only light in the interior of the plane was the red light, which at the right time would change to green as the signal to jump. In the darkness, each man was left to his own thoughts, trying not to dwell upon the possibilities of a bad landing – broken legs, snapped ankles, or worse – some of which they'd seen happen to fellow paratroopers at one time or another. Overwhelmed by adrenalin and almost unable to move, the soldiers placed their faces on their hands and retreated into a kind of semi-conscious catnap.

Drowning Creek

The plane Leon and the training team were in was a small, twin-engined cargo plane known as a CASA-212, in civilian markings but specially modified for covert military use. Due to the low altitude, the upper half of the cargo hatch was not even entirely closed. The plane flew a circuitous route to intentionally confuse the trainees.

There was a glow visible over the top of the cargo ramp as the plane passed over the edge of the Raleigh-Durham-Chapel Hill urban sprawl. Then things took on a science-fiction aspect as they flew by the massive cooling towers of the Sharon Harris nuclear power plant, the fantastic lightscape of the industrial complex below.

This too faded, and now there was only blackness beyond the open portion of the cargo hatch. They were flying over the thick Carolina pine forests, with only pinpoints of light as they passed the occasional farmhouse or cars moving along the unlit country roads.

In his role as jumpmaster, Leon got to his feet, hooked his static line to the anchor line cable and faced the team to begin the sequence of jump commands. The troops were jarred back to reality as the plane banked, climbed and dipped down, following the nap of the Earth at low altitude, in order to notionally evade 'enemy' radar. The momentum of increased G forces added to the troops misery as they struggled to their feet, aided by the crewmember, and then hooked their static lines to the anchor line cable and made a bight in their static lines. The troops checked their static lines, and the static lines of the man in front of them, to ensure they would not become entangled. A misrouted static line on exit from the aircraft could be catastrophic.

Leon turned to face the rear cargo hatch, now fully open, and moved onto the cargo ramp. He held the internal frame of the aircraft to brace himself as he looked down for the ground-to-air signal on the drop zone. In the darkness, Leon could barely make out landmarks. Knowing the actual route of the aircraft, he roughly knew where he was, and was able to recognize a large black area as Mott Lake, and long dark line that was Plank Road, against the subtle grays that was the pine forest all around. The drop zone was coming up. Leon turned, made a signal of his thumb and forefinger about an inch apart, and hollered,

"THIRTY SECONDS!"

Then he turned and faced the blackness beyond the cargo ramp. He felt the cold wind on his face and blowing his collars up against his neck. Leon's right hand was over the ripcord grip of his reserve parachute, to prevent an accidental opening – which could be fatal – his left hand holding his static line down and away, to ensure that it did not wrap around any part of his body – arm, leg, or neck. Paratroopers sometimes get dragged behind the plane after exit by a static line snagged somehow around their equipment, rucksack or rifle. The consequences are never good.

Leon leaned out to look ahead of the track of the aircraft one more time. Way down below a tiny set of lights appeared, in the pattern of an arrow. Leon looked up at the small red light by the top of the cargo ramp hatch. The red light went out and the green light below it came on. Leon looked over his shoulder and hollered "FOLLOW ME!" Then he turned, tucked his chin onto his chest and stepped off the cargo ramp into the blackness, the icy blast and the horrible drop.

Drowning Creek

* * *

The soldiers drifted down beneath the canopies of their parachutes, noiselessly in the dark, moonless night. The aircraft they'd exited from had feathered its props, rendering it nearly silent. The only sound was muffled thumps as the heavily equipped paratroopers landed, an occasional rustling of leaves as they moved towards the pre-planned assembly area. Despite careful study of their intended drop zone prior to take off, a crosswind had blown their chutes off the DZ. That, and because of the inky darkness, it took the team almost an hour to assemble.

Leon waited at the planned assembly point on the north edge of the drop zone, holding his compass facing south so that its luminescence would provide a visual signal to the other troops as they moved towards him.

Movement through the thick vegetation was arduous. They struggled against branches, thorn bushes and 'wait-a-minute' vines to make it to the assembly point. Each man carried at least seventy-five pounds on his back – the two radiomen had the heaviest rucksacks, almost thirty pounds more – plus their individual weapons, web gear, water and ammunition. On top of all their personal gear, each man brought his parachute off the drop zone, rolled up into an aviator's kit bag.

A slight glow in the eastern sky – the false dawn, before the dawn – signaled the early morning was approaching. At the edge of a wide-open area, just within the tree line, they formed a perimeter, all rifles pointing out. Leon instructed them to dump their parachutes in the center of the perimeter.

The fact the trainees had managed to safely un-ass the bird at low altitude, land and recover their gear, then assemble on the barely visual glow of his compass, reassured Leon that the men had their wits about them. Fortunately, no one was injured.

Once everyone was in place and they'd accounted for their weapons and sensitive items – radios and night vision devices – Leon spoke up, breaking the tactical silence. "Ok, we're going admin for a minute. I've got to put out some info, the situation has changed." He clicked on a white flashlight and threw a map on the ground. "As you are aware by now, there are many aspects of this training course that we do not communicate to you candidates. We want to assess how you deal with the unknown, and you've just been thrown a big curve ball. Everybody gather round."

The curious team moved around the map. Leon spoke up, "Team leader, do you know where you are on the map?"

The team leader studied the map for a moment, his brow furrowed. His hand moved over the map, locating the airfield they'd taken off from, then he pointed to a clearing to the west of the Camp Mackall cantonment area, the landing zone they'd briefed in their plan. "Here."

"No," Leon replied. "That's where you were supposed to jump into, but during our infil flight the plane was notionally taking heavy fire from the ground and the pilot had to take evasive action. He dropped us prematurely and turned back, skedaddled out of there. We are now here," he pointed to a clearing to the east of Camp Mackall, completely out of the area of operations they'd concentrated on during their planning. "Like I said, the situation has changed."

Leon gave the team a moment to digest this new information, then continued, "The mission has been scrubbed, there are no guerrillas here for you to link up with. You're on your own, and you are deep within enemy territory. Your only mission now is to move towards your pre-planned evasion corridor and evade out of here, back to friendly lines. This will require you to make movement through Fort Bragg – which is enemy territory – all the way back to the main base cantonment area, which is a friendly host country across the international border." Leon traced his finger across the map. "About thirty miles to the east of where we now are."

There was a collective groan from the team, sitting in the cold darkness. "But wait, it gets better," Leon went on. "The area between here and Fort Bragg is being heavily patrolled by platoon and squad sized elements from the 82nd Airborne Division – who are actually the enemy's elite troops - and any one of them who rolls up a Special Forces student gets a four-day pass, in conjunction with a weekend. What are your questions?"

There were none. "Good," Leon said. "Now then, I know this sucks, but it could suck a whole lot more."

"It could rain and then we'd really love how much it sucks," mumbled one of the troops, repeating the Camp Mackall mantra.

"That's right," Leon replied. "Maybe we'll all get lucky and the rain will freeze and then it will suck even more. But before I send you on your merry little way, I have a little gift for you."

The team eyeballed Leon warily. "This is not a test, your test was your team brief back," Lean said, "and I'm glad to inform you that you passed with flying colors. Good work."

Leon continued. "This part of the field training exercise isn't about dropping you off into the middle of a suckfest and setting you up for failure. I'm your instructor and advisor and I want you guys to succeed. Team leader, how do you expect to get past all those hardcore paratroopers from the 82nd Airplane Gang?"

"Well, we'll move tactically," the captain stated, "only move at night, practice noise and light discipline, hooch up by day, only cross streams and trails at bends to limit chances of enemy observation by fifty percent."

"Not bad, but you know those guys have got NODs* right? That, and they know this A.O. like the backs of their hands. You are literally in their backyard. There are hundreds of them combing the woods out there and they've all got a hard-on to roll you guys up. So what are you going to do?"

"Uh," the captain muttered, unsure how to answer.

"Um-hmm," Leon affirmed. "Well, I can't tell you WHAT to do, but I can advise you what I WOULD do if I was in your shoes." Leon pointed to the map. "This is Plank Road. It runs west to east all the way to where it becomes Chicken Road, and then leads right to Third Group and USASOC Headquarters – which just so happens to be the friendly lines you want to move towards. Plank Road is the southern boundary of Fort Bragg. You cannot go off post – it's fenced off, for one thing, and halfway to post it gets too built up with streets and neighborhoods to be able to maneuver through, anyway. Your evasion corridor is the narrow strip of land to the north of Plank Road." Leon pointed to a large area directly to the north of their evasion corridor. "Now what's this?"

"Uh, the impact area?"

---

* Night Observation Devices

Drowning Creek

The impact area was where all the artillery, mortars and aviation bombs were directed. On the map it was overprinted in gray, outlined in thick, dashed red lines.

"That's right," Leon said. "Can the 82d go there?" Leon asked.

"No," the captain replied.

"That's right. Now then, can Special Forces go there?"

"Hell, no!"

"Why not?"

"We'll get blown up!"

"Sure, there's a hazard if you go through the middle of the damn place. But what about sneaking into the impact area, just about one hundred and fifty meters or so, then moving out along a straight eastward azimuth?"

"But isn't that cheating?" one of the guys asked.

"Hey," Leon answered, "This is Special Forces. How does that saying go?"

"If you ain't cheatin', you ain't tryin'," the guys replied in a quiet chorus.

"That's right," Leon grinned. "Now how's the other part of the saying go?"

"If you get caught, you ain't tryin' hard enough."

"That's right," Leon said. "We're training for combat, and the difference between combat and sport is rules. If there are rules, it's a game. In a fight, if you're not cheatin' you're not tryin' hard enough to win.

"Like I said, I can't tell you what to do, but I'm telling you what I would do, if I was in your shoes. I want you guys to succeed, and the last thing I want to do listen to some asshole platoon sergeant from the 82nd woofing shit at some bar downtown Fayetteville about how he fucked up a bunch of my guys."

With that, Leon straightened up, folded the map and handed it to the team's captain, and snapped off his flashlight. "That's all I got gentlemen," he said. "Now I need to get out of here. My ride's waiting for me on the road, I'll be taking the 'chutes back with me. Good luck making it past the 82d, and I'll be waiting for y'all at the Bronze Bruce statue in front of USASOC Headquarters, bright and early Thursday morning. Be there or be square."

* * *

As Leon suggested, CID planted the ruse – the bit about getting the wives together for a spousal support group meeting – and Haglin took the bait. Ivy was visiting her mother up in New York, he said, she'll be gone for a couple weeks, maybe a month or more. "Oh really?" they said, "Then you may be interested to know we just fished her out of Drowning Creek. You're coming with us, down to headquarters."

When he heard this news, Leon's reaction was a mental *'Aw, shit.'* Haglin was a good officer, in some ways more human than the rest, and Leon honestly hated to see him go down like this. Knowing Ivy, Leon could only imagine how she'd driven him to it. The bitch was that crazy, and Leon was sorry Haglin had ever had anything to do with her.

Leon was thinking he should have spoken up at the wedding, when the pastor said that bit about if anyone has anything to say, let him now speak or forever hold his peace. '*Ah well*' Leon thought, '*Would've, could've, should've.*'

V

Leon wasn't surprised when word came down that Haglin wanted to see him. They were holding him in the brig at Camp Lejeune, awaiting trial, so bright and early the next morning Leon set off.

The drive from Bragg to Lejeune is a long and boring two and a half hours of secondary roads through flat farmland divided by stands of pine trees. There is no freeway, and there is no end of doublewide trailers with derelict cars and miscellaneous machinery rusting out front. Leon wanted to make the drive as early in the morning as possible to avoid any traffic that might lengthen the punishment, do his business at Lejeune, then get the hell out of there and back to civilization as soon as possible. Not that 'FayetteNam' is much in the way of civilization, but in some ways its better than Jacksonville. In other ways it's much worse, of course.

Along the way Leon had plenty of time to think – as unpleasant as it was to dwell on this thing. Leon had known Rudy Haglin for the better part of a decade. When Haglin had come to the team as a young captain, they'd lived together, worked and partied together for over two years, on three continents. They'd been through tight spots together. When soldiers work that close together, after a while they get to know one another so well that they can identify each other at a distance in the dark, just from the way they walk. Leon considered Haglin a friend, he was even at the wedding when Rudy married Ivy, although he had kept his distance after that. He didn't even go to the reception, and he sure as hell wasn't looking forward to seeing Rudy now, under the circumstances.

Leon had dropped a soldier off at the brig before so he knew what to expect. The Marines at the front desk are no nonsense. The way they looked at him and the vibe they put off, Leon felt like they considered him to be as much a criminal as the man he'd come to visit. He had to go through a search train, and was then escorted into the secure side of the brig, into an interview room. They brought in Rudy all shackled up like he was Public Enemy Number One.

"It's OK," Leon told the Marine who'd brought him in. "You can uncuff him."

"Uh, it's . . ." the kid started to say.

"I said uncuff him, Lance Corporal." Time to pull some rank. The Marine unlocked Haglin's chains, then left the room.

"Thanks," Rudy smiled, wanly.

"I wish I could do more," Leon said, and he meant it.

"Yeah," Rudy shrugged. It totally sucked for Leon to see the man like this. In all of the more than ten years he'd known Rudy Haglin, he'd never seen him looking as downhearted and crestfallen as he looked right now, and it was heart wrenching. Rudy had called for Leon and so he'd showed up, but if it were up to him, Leon wasn't sure he could have brought himself to see Rudy – not under the circumstances - and he sure as hell didn't know what to say.

Rudy opened the conversation by rolling up his sleeves and holding up his forearms in front of him. Leon's eyes went wide - Rudy's forearms were covered with red slashes. It looked like a guy he'd once seen who'd been in a serious knife fight –

Rudy's forearms were totally crisscrossed with fresh cuts, not even scarred over yet. He was practically cut to ribbons.

Leon's jaw dropped. "What. The. Fuck, sir? . . . Ivy?"

"Ivy."

"Well, I guess there's your defense," Leon said. "Self-defense, obviously."

"Yep."

"The only thing you fucked up was dumping her body in the creek."

"Yeah," Rudy smiled weakly. "I guess a guy does stupid stuff, under a stress like that."

"I guess," Leon shrugged. Indicating the cuts on his forearms, he asked, "This is why you wanted to see me?"

"Yes. I wanted you to know what happened, wanted you to see it for yourself. Let the guys in Group know that I'm not a total monster."

"What the fuck was going on, that Ivy turned on you and did a thing like this?"

Rudy drew a deep breath, then he started to tell his story.

"Being married to Ivy wasn't easy, right from the start."

Leon held back from commenting, the time had long come and gone to say anything about that.

"Right from the start there was tension, there were fights. I guess all couples have conflict, but I mean throwing things, crazy shit like that. But we'd always make up and things would be sweet and hunky dory again. Then it'd be some other thing.

It was like she had two personalities, almost, and there was an on/off switch."

"You're saying she was bipolar, or something?"

"No, it was more than that. There was something going on with Ivy. It was like she was leading a double life. In fact, that's exactly what it was."

"What do you mean?"

"Well, when we were dating she'd hidden her drug use from me."

This didn't exactly surprise Leon. He knew Ivy was a tramp but he didn't know much about her other than that. He did know she used blow – she'd said as much more than once, in the team room.

"On top of that, Ivy was a bit of a night owl, and she had her circle of friends. A couple of the girls she hung out with were strippers."

"Why am I not surprised?"

"Yeah, the usual cream of Fayetteville society."

Most G.I.'s see Fayetteville, North Carolina as an armpit where the dregs of society feed off the G.I.'s at the adjacent military base. A sort of symbiotic relationship. Numbers-wise, Fort Bragg is the largest base in the U.S. - there are more soldiers based at Fort Bragg than most countries have in their entire armies. These troops need diversion and entertainment, and Fayetteville delivers. Bars and strip clubs line Bragg Boulevard, intersected with tattoo parlors, pawn shops and used car lots that advertise "Good Credit / Bad Credit / No Credit – We Finance E-1 and Up!" which means they'll sell you a lemon at usury rates. Once, after the Iraq invasion, a pissed off G.I. rolled a grenade under a Corvette at one of these rip-off joints. Further out on the outskirts of town are the massage parlors, which are actually brothels.

A tier up from the topless bars and the red-light action is the bar scene where local girls flock in hopes of landing a G.I., which for a girl from the wrong side of the tracks means decent housing and healthcare, if she plays her cards right. It's a two-way street - G.I. Joe could win prizes for the things he marries. The situation can get quite feral on weekends.

But the place isn't a total cesspool. There are good and decent people in Fayetteville, there are probably more than the average number of churches for a city its size, and its schools and universities have produced their fair share of business success stories and athletic champions. But there's plenty acreage in the fabric of Fayetteville society for the seedier side of humanity to weave itself into. This was the environment that Ivy had emerged from.

Rudy went on. "I had reason to suspect Ivy was running around on me." Leon remained silent. "So I put a tail on her."

Green Berets don't have to hire private investigators, at least not in the Fort Bragg area. There is an unofficial underground network - clandestine surveillance operations are easy to set up. There's a lot of skullduggery that goes on around Fayetteville, and Special Forces soldiers have a unique skill set that lets them keep a finger on the pulse of things.

"Let me guess," Leon asked, "former boyfriend?" Hell, knowing Ivy, Leon half expected Rudy to come back with pimp, or something.

Drowning Creek

"No, actually," he said. "It was something different. Ivy was hanging out with a bunch of guys, over at their place."

Leon sure as hell didn't want to hear where this was going – images of Ivy and her stripper friends doing orgies flashed across his mind - but Rudy surprised him.

"It's not what you're thinking," he said. "I was thinking the same thing at first – that she was having some kind of affair, some kind of side action. But it wasn't that."

"What was it?"

"You remember that guy down in Colombia? Ex-FARC guy, working with us and the DEA, we all called him *Capitán Gato* because he looked like a cat?"

"Hell yeah, I remember Gato!" Leon replied. "He was always slinking around everywhere, ingratiated himself into everything, just like a fucking stray cat that shows up and never goes away!"

"That's right," Rudy went on. "Somehow that Gato guy got himself assigned to us as a sort of unofficial liaison. Every single damn thing of any significance that we did down there, Gato would show up."

"I never trusted that fucker an inch," Leon said. "Especially after I saw his pic on the Wall of Shame, in that bar Bogota where the contractors and all the wannabe mercenaries hung out."

"Well, this is going to sound really weird, but the guys who were pulling surveillance on Ivy came back with some pics, and who do you think was going in and out of this house where Ivy was hanging out at?"

"You gotta be kidding me. Gato?"

"I kid you not."

"There always was something about Capitán Gato that rubbed me the wrong way."

"Exactly" Rudy said. "The guy's a snake."

"What the fuck is Gato doing up here, in Fayetteville?"

"That is exactly what I was wondering. Right away I started thinking – what the hell WOULD he be doing. It couldn't be anything good."

"Some kind of exchange program? Embedded training with the U.S. Army?"

"That doesn't make sense. State and the Department of Defense vet the hell out of those guys – just like their people vet us. Think about it. There's no way they're going to let an ex-FARC, ex-communist guerrilla turd like Gato come anywhere near Fort Bragg, in any kind of official capacity."

"Then, what?" Leon asked.

"I went to C.I." Counter-Intelligence. "Told them what I had, all about Gato, and asked them what they thought about that, asked them what the hell would a snake like Gato doing in Fayetteville, home to thousands of Special Forces soldiers, Delta, JSOC, the entire 82d Airborne Division and the Eighteenth Airborne Corps."

"And?"

"As far as I know, they sat on it. The guy I spoke to said, "How do you know this guy is who you're saying he is?" He said he had nothing to go on, no start point."

"He probably said that in order to keep a lid on it," Leon offered, "to let you think nothing's going on so that you can't blow the lid on any kind of investigation that IS going on."

"Hmmm, I never thought of that."

"Yeah, there's always a deception plan, a deception within a deception, and a deception on top of that. These Spy-versus-Spy guys live in the fucking Wilderness of Mirrors. You know, Tinker-Tailor-Soldier-Spy, all that spooky stuff."

"Yeah, I guess so," Rudy said, looking down.

"So what did you do about it?" Leon asked.

"Well, you know how they tell us to never to do a James Bond act, to just report and then back off, right?"

"Let me guess," Leon asked. "You did a James Bond act?"

"Well, not exactly, but I did step up the surveillance. If the C.I. guys weren't going to do anything about it, then I had to get more intell. I needed something that was going to light a fire under their asses, and hell, I needed to know what the hell my wife was up to."

Rudy continued. "I told the guys to lay real low, that the thing with Ivy was entering a critical stage. I insisted that the guys rotate out so they didn't set any patterns. I didn't tell anyone my suspicions about Gato - his being up here in the first place was shady as fuck, in and of itself. The guys just thought they were collecting for an upcoming divorce case. Happens all the time in Fayetteville."

"We got photos of Gato coming and going, and his team of henchmen," Rudy continued. "What a shady crew – they couldn't be up to anything good. Meanwhile I'm wondering what the fuck Ivy's doing with this pack of international shitheads?"

"Did you find anything out?"

"I'm not really sure. I found out enough to get my hackles up. These guys are coming and going and we got some pretty good pics of all of them. This is where it gets strange and weird."

"What do you mean?"

"I was up in Raleigh," Rudy went on, "part of this project I was on. We wanted to bring the Army-Navy game down to Raleigh-Durham area. You know it's always up by DC, or around Annapolis, or Philly, or New York. Well, a bunch of us officers who graduated from UNC and Duke and Wake Forest wanted to bring the game down here for once, and I was point man in trying to arrange things. Coming back, I stopped at this no name gas station, off of Highway One - Deep River Road, south of the Deep River about halfway between Raleigh and Pinehurst, out in the middle of nowhere."

"I know that place," Leon said. "The place with the grass growing up through the cracks in the pavement, all around the pumps."

"Yeah. Well, I filled up my tank, then went inside to get a bottle of Gatorade. The two guys behind the counter were some kind of Middle Easterners – Pakistanis or Iranians or something, they weren't Arabs, as far as I could tell.

"So I'm paying for my Gatorade and my bag of chips, and now there's four of the guys – they could have been brothers, they all looked alike – and they were chattering on like a house on fire. It wasn't Arabic, it sounded like Farsi, or Pashtu, or Urdu – I don't speak any of those languages, just a bit of Arabic.

Then I look over to the door to the backroom they're coming in and out of and all of a sudden fucking Gato walks out."

"No shit?"

"I shit you not."

"What did you do?"

"I ducked my head low and got the fuck out of there, but I'm pretty damn sure Gato got a look at me. How could he not? I was the only customer in the joint."

"What do you think's going on?"

"I don't know, but when I got home I looked at the pics I had of the crew at the house Ivy was going in and out of, and I'll be damned if I didn't recognize these assholes right off the bat. They were the same bunch I'd seen that afternoon at the No-Name gas station, on Deep River Road, off of Highway One."

"What do you think's going on?" Leon asked again.

"I don't know, but then Ivy came in the door. She sidled over and looked at what I was looking at. I tried to play it cool, like I was shuffling through some paperwork but she'd seen these 8x10 black and whites I was looking at and right away she's like, 'what have you got there?'

"I'm like, 'oh nothing, honey' and tried to play the whole thing off but I was obviously busted and my adrenalin is pumping, right? So I'm shaking as I'm trying to stuff the pics back into this manilla envelope, meanwhile Ivy comes around the table, and when she saw what I was looking at she went totally ape shit."

"I bet."

"The thing escalated so fast. 'You're spying on me!' she yells. 'Well, yeah,' I say, 'you're hanging out with all these assholes!' 'You fucking asshole!' she yells. Then she's hitting me. I'm putting my arms up and blocking her blows and of course I'm not hitting back because a domestic spouse abuse is the kiss of death for one of us, right? Even if it's self-defense. And besides, I've got nothing against her, I don't want to hurt her."

Leon just grunted at this. Rudy went on. "Then she gets real quiet, and I'm telling you she was so cool and quiet it chilled me to the fucking bone. Ivy turned her back on me and for a second I thought okay, it's over. Then she turns and comes at me with a straight razor in her hand, slashing the air with the damn thing and coming straight at me."

"Holy fucking shit!"

"Yeah! A fucking straight razor!" Rudy exclaimed. "Well now I'm trying to defend myself, and I'm taking all kinds of cuts," he indicated his forearms, "and she's slashing away at me, and I swear I was afraid for my life!"

Leon thought of how he'd encountered Steve with his throat slashed, years ago, and at that point he thought Rudy Haglin had every reason in the world to be afraid of Ivy, armed with a straight razor in her hand.

"So you killed her." It was a statement, not a question.

"I finally got a hold of her wrist, the hand that was holding the straight razor, but there was blood all over my hands and I couldn't get a good grip, it was slippery as hell, like it was coated with 30-weight oil. My other hand I put around her throat and just squeezed. She was a fucking wild animal and there wasn't any way to stop her. I just squeezed like hell because my grip on her wrist was slipping and she was trying to kill me with that damn straight razor of hers.

"Then her eyes bulged out and she went limp and it was over."

Rudy was looking at the table in front of him. He was breathing hard, almost sobbing, as he relived that moment.

Leon finally spoke up. "You know, if you'd have just called the cops after that, none of this would be happening right now."

"I know. I fucked up." Then he shrugged his shoulders. "It is what it is."

Things were quiet for a while, then Leon spoke up. "Is there anything I can do for you?"

"There is, actually. A lot."

"Name it."

"Go to my place. The photos I told you about are in a strongbox in the closet in the room I use for an office. The key is on a keychain in a drawer downstairs in the kitchen – you'll see it. Get the photos, go to C.I., go to the FBI, go to the C.I.D., go to whoever – anybody and everybody - and tell them what I told you, and alert them onto these assholes. Gato doesn't belong here, he's totally out of place, he's hanging out with these Middle Eastern dudes and whatever the hell it is they are up to, it's crazy enough to have set Ivy off enough to try to kill me over it."

"I'll do it, man."

"Thank you."

There was no way Leon could say no to Rudy Haglin. A guy he considered a friend was going to be sent up the river for what was basically an act of self-defense against his crazy bitch wife Ivy and her straight razor, and all this weirdness seemed to somehow be driven by a cabal of Iranians or Pakistanis or whatever the fuck they were, and that snake Gato was somehow in the middle of it all.

VI

Leon had plenty of food for thought as he drove back to Bragg. When he got back to town his first stop was to swing by Rudy's place to look for the pics Rudy had told him about. Leon picked the lock, let himself in, and punched the number combo Rudy had given him to the security system: 1-2-3-4, of all things. How stupid is that?

Leon got a weird feeling as he moved around Rudy's place, looking at the plaque they'd given Rudy when he left the team, wedding pics of Rudy and Ivy, pics of the loving couple on vacation at some place in the tropics. The loving couple - that made Leon feel creepy as fuck. He found the pics – they were right where Rudy said they were, in the strong box, in one of those manila envelopes that closes with a little piece of string going around a circular bit of card.

Leon spread the pics out on the coffee table and looked at them. Black and white glossies, 8 x 10's. The front of a house in a suburban neighborhood - it looked like Fayetteville, but it could really be anywhere in the south – with a white van parked in the driveway. Another shot, this one with another white van on the street in front of the place. There were some guys who looked like they might have been South Americans, or some kind of Middle Easterners - Leon recognized Gato.

Looking around the room, Leon spotted a woman's handbag. Probably Ivy's. He picked it up and dumped the contents out on the coffee table. There was a purse with Ivy's ID, credit cards and cash, some cosmetics, a small tin that was obviously

Ivy's weed stash, and a set of keys. There was a separate key with a solid plastic back end to it, on a solid key ring that almost looked like a grenade pin, with a thick plastic tag engraved with a number.

Leon held the key up and studied it for a moment. It appeared to be a key to one of those rental lockers they have at airports, bus stations or bowling alleys. Then he put the key into his pocket, pulled out his wallet, took out the card the C.I.D. agent Johnson had given him and gave him a call.

Leon went and opened the door and sat down on a chair in the living room where he could see the door and tooled through his phone while he waited for Johnson to show up. Glancing up, Leon saw a guy coming to the door holding a Beretta 92FS in both hands – the pistol was pointed at the ground, thank God – and a wild-eyed look on his face, mouth in a circle like an 'O'.

"WOAH!" Leon yelled, showing the guy his hands.

"Who the fuck are YOU!?" the guy hollered, "WHO THE FUCK ARE YOU!?" starting to bring the pistol up.

"I'm a friend of Haglin's!" Leon hollered back, holding his hands higher. "Who the fuck are YOU?"

"I'm his neighbor," the guy said, lowering the pistol and decocking it. "I saw a strange car on the driveway and noticed the door wide open. I haven't seen Rudy or Ivy for a couple of days so I figured he was away. So I thought I'd check and see, make sure some Fayetteville punks weren't ripping him off."

Leon's head was spinning. For a split second his heart had stopped but now it was racing too fast to say anything

Drowning Creek

sensible. Thank God the guy didn't shoot first, ask questions later.

"I can show you some ID if you like. C.I.D. are already on their way, if you want to sit and wait."

"That's OK, I'll take your word for it," he said. "You don't look like a Fayetteville punk, and besides, you know Rudy's name."

Crisis averted. *'Always something fucked up happening in FayetteNam,'* Leon thought.

Johnson finally showed up. Leon showed him inside.

"Whaddya got?"

"Sit down, this is going to take a while."

Leon recounted what Rudy had said, all about the situation with Ivy - how he'd put surveillance on her and found out about the creepy guys she was hanging out with. Leon told Johnson what Rudy had told him about the confrontation with Ivy, and the cuts all over his forearms. Then Leon told him about Gato, how Gato showed up on the scene in Fayetteville of all places, and the scene at the No-Name gas station out on Deep River Road. Then Leon showed him the 8x10 black and white pics of Ivy getting out of her car at the house, the Middle Easterners coming and going, and Gato. Leon put my finger on him. "That's him. That's Gato."

"You know this guy?"

"Yes. Everybody on my team knows Gato. Half of Special Forces knows Gato. Whenever we went down south, he was there. The guy was like a bad rash, you couldn't shake him."

"What does any of this have to do with Haglin killing his wife?"

"I don't know, but I know Rudy Haglin, and I knew Ivy, and I know this Gato fucker. Something's going on, but I don't know what. None of this stuff is adding up. Yet."

"What are you trying to do? Get Haglin off the hook?"

"No. I'm just telling you what I've learned – stuff you may or may not already know. I don't know what Haglin told you guys, but the cuts on his arms alone ought to be enough to get him off the hook."

"He didn't say anything," Johnson said. "He just said he wanted to talk to a lawyer."

"I don't blame him for that."

"You Green Berets always clam up. It's that resistance to interrogation training they give you. The only time I've seen one of you guys start talking is when we got this one guy dead to rights, and he started blabbering his head off."

"Haglin wasn't talking, what's that tell you?"

"I dunno," Johnson said. "It's weird, because he's as guilty as sin."

"Is he? What is he guilty of? Dumping the body in the creek was stupid – and criminal – but the slashes on his forearms, that tells me it was self-defense."

"He could have done those to himself."

"I was thinking of that when I looked at them," Leon answered. "Not very likely. The placement of those cuts on his arms - they were deep, thin, clean slices - at angles a guy couldn't do to himself. Anyway," he went on, "You need to put this into your investigation."

"What for? Haglin killed his wife, choked her to death with his bare hands, and then dumped her body in the creek. We caught him out in a lie about his wife being away to visit his mother, what's there to investigate?"

"Absolutely there's something to investigate. The cuts all over his arms suggest it was self-defense."

"You think Ivy was capable of doing such a thing?"

"I know she was."

"What makes you say that?"

"Remember how I told you all about my guy Steve Meisinger?" Leon reminded Johnson, "About bumping into Ivy at the hospital, her skedaddling out of there in one hell of a hurry just before I walked into Steve's room and found him there with his throat slit and blood all over the place?"

"Oh yeah," Johnson acknowledged. "That."

"Yeah, that," Leon shot back. "When I saw those cuts all over Haglin's arms, I knew he was telling the truth about Ivy. The woman is more than capable of slashing a guy up with a straight razor. Or was, I should say," Leon corrected himself.

"For a guy who's trying to distance himself from this thing, you sure have a lot to say about it," Johnson said.

"Shit," Leon replied, "All I'm saying is Haglin killed Ivy, I'm sure of it, but I'm also pretty damn sure it was self-defense."

"Well, you sure seem to be digging your way in," Johnson said.

"Wouldn't you? All I'm trying to do is help a friend. Hell, first time we spoke, you guys were trying to suggest I had something to do with it."

"You call me up and lay out this whole scenario," Johnson indicated the pics on the table between us, "What have you got to do with all of this?"

"Nothing. I'm not in the middle of all this." Leon pointed at Gato, in one of the pics. "This guy. I don't know what his connection is with Ivy, and I don't know what he's up to, and I don't know who the hell all these Middle Eastern looking assholes are, but somewhere in there is the reason why Ivy went off and came at Rudy with her straight razor."

"You think there's some kind of international intrigue going on here?"

"Why would there not be? This is Fort Bragg – we know the bad guys are here in Fayetteville already, watching us, watching everything that happens around this place, keeping their fingers on the pulse of America's 9-1-1 force. Hell, everybody knows that if all the pizza joints on Yadkin Road start delivering a ton of pizzas to Eighteenth Airborne Corps headquarters at one in the morning, some miserable third world dictator is about to have the 82nd Airborne drop in on his ass. But this has got to be more than that, more than just keeping eyes-on all the Green Berets and the paratroopers."

"I don't know if this is going to make any difference for Haglin, other than the cuts on his arms suggest he killed her in self-defense," Leon went on. "What gets me is something set Ivy off, drove her to try and kill her husband. Whatever it is, it's got to be pretty big. Significant, I'd say."

Drowning Creek

"Well, if you do think there's some kind of international espionage thing going on, you need to talk to C.I., not us." Counter-Intelligence - the Spy versus Spy guys, the spy catchers.

"I know," Leon said. "That's who I'm talking to next. I just want all this documented – what I told you, where I found all this shit," Leon indicated the pics with his chin.

"How do we know you didn't set this all up, trying to get your friend off the hook?"

"What? C'mon, are you serious?" Leon said, incredulous. "What kind of stagecraft would THAT take? Lemme see here – I've got to find this Gato cat, and a pack of Iranian beardo-weirdos, get pics of them, develop them, then call you up to show them to you – where would I find the time to do that, since yesterday? In between pulling Ivy out of the creek and then talking to you guys, then doing a night jump with a bunch of trainees, then waking up early and driving all the way out to Lejeune and back? There isn't time enough in the day."

"Yeah, I guess so," Johnson admitted.

"I bet you'd find Haglin's prints on these glossies, anyway," Leon said. "How the hell could I arrange that, after the fact?"

"Who took all these pics, anyway?"

"Fellow Green Berets. I'll ask Haglin – or you can. I think it's pretty important to know. Now do me a favor and document everything I told you, and you can come with me when I talk to C.I. if you like. In fact, I'd prefer that, because it'd give this whole thing a lot of credibility."

"Well, I . . ." Johnson stammered.

"Well, what? You've got something more important than trying to figure out why a cabal of international bad guys drove an SF Team Queen to try and kill her husband? Must be pretty damn important, whatever it is."

"I guess you're right. Before we go to C.I., we're going to have to go to your unit, let your G-2 know. You've got to keep your chain of command informed, before you go flying off into the middle of an investigation that's starting to grow arms and legs like an octopus."

"No time like the present," Leon said. He was beginning to wonder, '*What's it take to light a fire under this guy's ass? Where the hell is everyone's sense of urgency?*' "Besides," he pointed out, "who knows what's up with these assholes? Be no good if they all go to ground, now that Ivy's out of the picture."

"Let's go."

VII

Leon and Johnson went over to the S-2 offices, behind Group Headquarters. A young soldier ushered them into an inner office, where an ornate desk piece announced who they were in the presence of, in large, hand carved wooden letters: CAULFIELD. A major's leaf affixed to the nameplate informed the world of his rank: Major Caulfield.

A bit on the plump side, sort of pink and freckly, Major Caulfield wasn't exactly Bond, James Bond, but Leon knew better than to underestimate a guy on his looks. Caulfield struck him as a prior-enlisted guy who'd climbed his way up to field grade rank by tooth and claw - he could be a careerist, an opportunist, a back-stabbing snake, or he could very well be hard-working, productive, resourceful, a supportive asset, an absolute shot in the arm. Leon had no way of knowing, he'd just have to roll the dice with this guy and find out.

It was what it was. Leon needed a start point with this mess, going forward, and this was it. Caulfield had a completely no-nonsense look on his face as Leon recounted what he'd told Johnson. Somehow, the story seemed to lack immediacy and intensity, telling it a third time. In fact, Leon was starting to feel like an idiot.

Then Leon reminded himself that this wasn't his story. He was telling it for Rudy, who at this very moment was cooling his heels in the brig – not a fun place even on a good day – and if there was any kind of way out of where Rudy was at and where he was going, Leon figured he was holding what might possibly be the key.

When Leon was done recounting the whole thing, Caulfield finally spoke, "That's it? That's all you got?"

"What more do you want?"

"You basically have nothing. A guy's wife – as you described her, a 'Team Queen' – is running around town. She's caught out by her husband, there's a fight, he kills her. End of story. Not the first time something like this has happened in Fayetteville. Won't be the last."

Leon's jaw dropped.

"What do you make of all this?" Caulfield looked at Johnson.

"About the same way you see it."

'*Jeez,*' Leon thought, '*this is going absolutely nowhere.*'

"Who took these photos?" Caulfield asked.

"I can find out," Leon replied. "Why is that important?"

"I'm going to have to write a report on all this, and I'll need as much information as possible. I can't just say there are some photos. I gotta know the who-what-where-when-why and how many."

"The who is easy enough'" Leon started. "Gato is already a known entity, and we know how many." Then he looked at Johnson, "If you do a little snooping around you might just find out all the rest of the five W's."

"If you had any idea how many false leads we have to chase down around here," Caulfield said. "This is just one more straw in a huge bale of hay that is our workload."

"Jeez, you sound like the guy telling the radar operators at Pearl not to worry about all those blips on the radar screen on the morning of December 7th," Leon said. "Isn't it your job to chase down shit like this?"

"Let me tell you my next move," Leon went on. "I'm going to find the best, most expensive lawyer I can find to help Rudy Haglin the best I can, and I'm going to get some photos of all those cuts on his forearms." Leon paused. "Tell you what else, I wouldn't mind if the Feds get involved in this shit, the FBI. In fact, I think I'm heading straight for the Federal building in Raleigh, right away. You can come with me if you like. In fact, I'd like the moral support." When nobody said anything, he stood up. "Standing around here talking is eating up a lot of time, so I'm getting started right now."

Caulfield looked at Johnson, Johnson looked at Caulfield, and then they both looked at Leon. "Sit down," Caulfield said. Leon sat down. "I can see you're pretty damn serious about this thing."

"Damn straight I'm serious. I think there's some serious shit going down. I wish you'd see it my way."

"Okay," Caulfield nodded, moving the pics on the desk around with his fingertips. "At this time, I'm going to suggest that you don't start snooping around on your own. The worst thing you can do is try to pull off a one-man cloak-and-dagger operation."

"I'm going to do what I gotta do, to find out what the hell is going on with these assholes, what drove Ivy to come at Haglin with her straight razor."

"You really believe what Haglin told you?"

"He isn't lying."

"How do you know he isn't lying?"

"I know the man like a brother. We worked, walked, talked together, ate, fought, chased girls together, you name it, for the better part of five years in some real choice shitholes. You get to know a guy pretty damn good under those circumstances. I can read Rudy Haglin like a book and I'd know if he was lying, because it'd be so hard for him to lie to a brother, it'd be as obvious as the day is long. Especially about a thing like this. What Rudy was telling me was no act. He was dead straight what he was talking about, straight as an arrow. It was no fucking act."

Caulfield and Johnson exchanged knowing looks.

"Consider," Leon said. "If he's lying, then he's just another piece of shit who killed his wife. Happens all the time, like you said. But if he isn't lying – and in his favor, there's the cuts all over his arms and what I told you just now – then there's something more to this than meets the eye. A LOT more. Something I think is in the best interests of the United States Army to find out."

"Go find a lawyer for Haglin," Caulfield said. "I'll hang on to these pics, make a file."

"Those are evidence," Johnson spoke up. "You can make photocopies, but those are part of an active investigation."

Leon could see real fast where all of this was going. An old sergeant major had once told him: "If you ever have to kill somebody, the best thing you can do is drag the body onto Fort Bragg and dump it. That way you've just crossed so many lines of jurisdiction – local, county, state, Federal and military

– that the investigators will be so busy stepping all over each other's toes, they'll never solve the killing."

This thing was starting to go into spin, and once it spun out of control Rudy's chances of beating this thing would only be so much splatter on the wall. The only chance Rudy had, Leon figured, the only chance of finding out whatever the hell it was that Gato was up to, was to get personally involved on an operational level. It was time to grab this thing by the stacking swivel, swing it around and take control of it.

"Okay," said Caulfield. "I'll make photocopies. In fact, I'll scan the damn things. Then I'll bring them to you."

Leon rolled his eyes - too many layers of bureaucracy creeping into this shit show. "I'm coming along," Leon said.

"Well, uh . . ."

"Think about it – what's better? I tell them, with my personal knowledge of the individuals concerned, or you tell them, third hand?"

"Okay," Caulfield nodded as he scooped the pics into back into their folder. "I guess that only makes sense. You busy right now?"

"No," said Leon. "In fact, I'm going to take some leave, because this thing is going to take a lot more time than I can squeak out of at work. There's no way I can track on this shit, chase this shit down if I'm running herd on a bunch of trainees out at Mackall. Besides, they won't miss me out there."

"Okay."

Caulfield was finally starting to come across as the resourceful, productive type. That was a relief. Last thing Rudy needed for the shit he was in was an office politician playing toad-in-the-road.

Caulfield looked at Johnson. Johnson looked at Caulfield, then both of them looked at Leon again. The meeting was over, it was time to move on to the next thing.

* * *

Leon drove into a drive-thru and got a cup of coffee. Sitting in his truck watching the parking lot through the raindrops falling on his windshield, Leon reflected on the bits and pieces of the situation. He felt inside his pocket and withdrew the key he'd taken from Ivy's handbag. The locker key. The large plastic fob had the number 32 engraved in it.

It occurred to Leon that there were only three places he knew of in Fayetteville that had these lockers – the airport, the bowling alley, and the bus station. Leon didn't think the locker this key fit into was at the bus station - that place was a combat zone, nobody went there if they could possibly avoid it. Most likely the airport. He'd swing by the bowling alley, try it, then hit the airport - it was on the way.

The key did not fit locker 32 at the bowling alley. Next stop, the airport. Viola, the key fit. Inside the locker was a plastic strong box, with snaps, O-ring sealed with an air pressure relief valve, like a gun box, only smaller. Glancing about with his hands still inside the locker, Leon popped the box open to have a peek.

Inside was a cylindrical device made of smoothly brush-polished steel, about seven inches long with a sleeve about it of similar machined steel. There were some tiny inscriptions, and a complex pattern of geometric lines. Most unusual was a sort of window or portal, of some kind of hardened glass - it seemed to be a display interface, a screen, but it was blank. The opposite side of the device had a similar panel, but of some kind of crystalline mineral, vivid blue and green, like opal. Leon had no idea what it could possibly be, but it had to be important - there was already one dead body associated with the thing.

Leon stuffed the box under his coat and walked out of the airport to where he'd parked his truck in the short-term parking lot. The whole way to his truck he felt like the damn thing was radioactive or something. The thing had a presence about it.

He dropped by Rudy's place on his way home and put the key back into Ivy's handbag. Whatever the damn thing was, if anybody was after it, let them go on a wild goose chase. When he got home, he went to the walk-in closet in his bedroom and stuffed the box with its mysterious object into the secret hole he'd carved through the sheetrock, just inside the inside wall of his walk-in closet, where nobody would ever think to look.

Leon went into his living room and looked inside his liquor cabinet. poured himself a stiff one. He hated to take a drink to settle his nerves but sometimes a drink was what was called for - it had been a long couple of days and he was done. His liquor cabinet was empty, of course. Resigned to sobriety, Leon kicked back into his leather sofa, clicked on the TV. Some stupid talking head was reporting on the 'Green Beret Murder'. Leon hit the mute button and tried to settle his thoughts, which were bouncing around the inside of his skull like a ping-pong ball in a popcorn machine.

VIII

The shit was piling up fast. Leon's priorities were to get a lawyer for Rudy, go with him to the brig at Lejeune as soon as possible and get pics of those cut marks all over Rudy's forearms while they were still fresh. The Marines who ran the brig wouldn't let Leon in with a phone when he went to see him. Maybe a lawyer could get a phone or at least a camera in.

Leon also needed to find out who Rudy had tailing Ivy and find out what they knew. He already knew the address of where Gato and his crew were hanging out because it was written on the notes that accompanied the pics. C.I. had the pics, but Leon had already taken pics of the pics and had everything he needed for a start point. Everything, that is, short of talking to the actual guys who took the pics.

But for now Leon needed to decompress, cool his jets. He headed down to a little hole in the wall bar he knew, off Fort Bragg Road, away from all the glitzy joints on Bragg Boulevard where the G.I.'s hung out in droves. Being a Tuesday night, he was hoping the place would be empty, and he'd get some time to talk to Jill, his favorite Fayetteville bartender.

The place was deserted. 'Thank God,' Leon thought as he took his place at the bar, he had no patience for crowds at this time. It was just himself, Jill behind the bar, and a beautiful young lady writhing under a blue light on the little dais that served for a stage in that place, at the far end of the bar. She was dancing to the saxophone solo of a classic Seventies rock tune.

Drowning Creek

Gyrating under the dim colored light, it was like her body was the living embodiment of the Blues.

Leon had once asked a stripper if she could move like that with her feet off the ground. She winked and told him, "Where do you think I learned it?"

Jill was wearing white lingerie that glowed fluorescent under the blacklight above the bar - bustier, string-sided panties, thigh-hi stockings and heels. Compared to the young lady wrapping herself around the stripper pole, Jill was fully clothed.

"Hello, Jill."

"Hello, Leon. What'll it be?"

"I'll have a Heineken, thanks. How are you doing?"

"I'm doing fine, thanks. Really good. And if you tip me right, I'll be doing even better."

In Fayetteville, people get down to the brass tacks early in the conversation. Leon pulled out his wallet and laid a twenty-dollar bill on the bar right in front of Jill. "Thank you, Leon," Jill smiled.

"How's the wife?" he asked. Jill was a Lesbian – she was in a married relationship with another woman.

"She's doing fine."

"And Sophie?"

"She's doing fine, too. She's in school now. Second grade."

"Wow. Time flies." Leon peeled off another two twenties. "Buy her some shoes or something."

"Thank you, Leon."

Looking over to the dancer, he asked, "Who's the new talent?"

"Nancy. She's working her way through college."

"Really? What's she studying?"

"Not sure. Something heavy. Quantum physics, or something like that."

"Ha! What do you know about quantum physics?"

"Not my field. What I know about is astronomy."

"Oh really?"

"Yeah, the powerful attraction of heavenly bodies."

"I love it."

Nancy finished her set, retrieved her bikini top, strapped it on and walked over to join Jill and Leon at the other end of the bar. To say she was beautiful would almost be an insult, the girl was a total knockout - a tall, slim, stunning brunette, very shapely with long legs, magical hips, a narrow waist and full, round breasts that were as solid and firm as only a young woman's breasts can be. She sat down next to Leon. "Hello," she said.

Leon struggled to keep his eyes above her neckline but it was not easy. *'Thank God for peripheral vision,'* he thought.

"Aren't you going to tip the dancer?" Jill asked. "Don't let the music fool you, this ain't the 1970s. The era of Free Love is over."

Leon peeled off a hundred-dollar bill and placed it on the bar in front of Nancy.

"Well, HELLO Handsome!" Nancy flashed a wide smile. "What's your name?"

"Uncle Benjamin," he said.

"Really?"

"Nancy, this is Leon," Jill interjected. "Leon, this is Nancy. Leon has obviously just come back from overseas. I don't know what it is they do over there, but they always come back richer than shit and horny as hell."

Nancy smiled at this cliche.

"It's a slow night," Leon shrugged. "I figure you gotta get paid for what you're doing, and if I wasn't in here right now you'd be making doodly squat tonight."

"Thank you," Nancy said as she tucked the hundred-dollar bill away into somewhere in her skimpy string bikini.

"Leon is one of the few gentlemen in this town," Jill said. "One of the last of a dying breed. He's not like those savages that infest those meat markets up there on the Boulevard."

Nancy smiled approvingly.

"You're in college?" Leon asked.

"Yeah."

"What do you study?"

"Computer science and technology."

"You should be studying economics."

"Why's that?"

"Because I could give you private tutoring, one-on-one," he said, peeling off another hundred and placing it on the bar in front of her.

Nancy put an elbow on the bar, leaned forward, holding up her head on her hand. "You know, you're turning into the most interesting person I've met in a long, long time," she said. "What do you do in the Army?" Her incredible cleavage was killing Leon, an overwhelming distraction.

"As little as possible. I'm a cook, actually."

"Yeah, right," said Jill.

"No, but I can cook."

"What can you cook?" Nancy asked.

"Anything. Everything. The usual stuff," Leon said. "Beer can chicken. Jambalaya."

"Mmmm, you're making me hungry. I've been working that pole all night."

"Yeah, it's been a long day and a night for me, too," Leon said. "Tell you what, I'll take you out for a late dinner, or an early breakfast if you like, when you get off."

Jill went into a back room, returned in jeans and a t-shirt. She walked around the bar, started putting chairs up on tables. "Get your clothes on, Nancy. It's Monday night, we're closing early. There ain't nobody else coming in here tonight."

"You serious about buying me dinner?" Nancy asked.

"Sure, why not? We can grab a bite to eat. How you getting' home?"

"Uber."

"Oh my God," Leon exclaimed. "Not in this town. Jill, you ain't taking care of this girl?"

"You can take care of her, Leon," Jill replied. Then to Nancy, "You're in safe hands with Leon, Nancy. In fact, if you go with Leon, you could not be safer."

Late at night on a rainy Monday, Fayetteville is almost civilized. You can get anything you want in Fayetteville, and tonight Leon was getting lucky. This was the kind of luck you pay for, of course, but like Jill said, the era of Free Love is over. They say you can't buy love, but you can rent it.

When they got to his place, Leon said, "I bet you would probably like to take a shower." This evoked a positive response, so he showed Nancy his room-sized, walk-in shower. He unloaded and cleared his pistol, an M1911 .45 caliber Government Model. He dropped the magazine, locked the slide to the rear, looked into the chamber, looked into the mag well to double make sure he'd dropped the mag, then looked into the chamber again – holding it up to the light just to make sure that what he'd seen the first time was exactly what he thought he'd seen and the chamber was empty – and then he stashed his pistol away.

Then Leon undressed and walked over to the bathroom door. Cracking the door a bit, he said "Can I come in?"

Without waiting her reply, Leon entered the streaming hot water. Nancy moved to make room for him. Leon stood behind her, put his arms about her to hold her close, moved his hands up to hold her breasts as he kissed her neck. Nancy was young and beautiful, her body soft, yet firm against his chiseled athletic frame. She reached down to find that he was already happy to see her. The warm water enveloped them as he gently massaged fragrant soap into her skin. The sound of cascading water mingled with their shared laughter, creating a symphony of intimacy. He moved his palms up and down her smooth curves, wordlessly acknowledging her beautiful body. Stepping out of the shower, they wrapped themselves in plush towels. The air was thick with a heady mix of steam and desire.

It was time to take it to the bedroom.

The soft glow of ambient light created an atmosphere of quiet passion. The bed with its pillows piled high and thick comforter was a haven, a sanctuary for two lovers and their unspoken desires. He traced the contours of her body with gentle fingertips, as if he was playing a tune on a fine instrument, a sweet melody only they could hear. She wrapped her legs about him and the rest of the world ceased to exist as their bodies moved together in a slow dance, the timeless rhythm of love. Embraced by the night, they lost themselves to a deep connection that transcended the physical, ascended to a spiritual sublime.

In the afterglow the lovers looked into one another's eyes. Nancy sensed a vulnerability beneath his rugged exterior, unaware of the secrets veiled by his profession. As for Leon, he found himself entangled in a delicate tempest of emotions, almost yearning for a connection beyond their physical encounter.

Falling in love is easy. Sex is easier. Finding someone who can spark your soul, that shit is rare. Leon found someone once – they found each other - but then she flew away. It was not meant to be. And so for now at least, this was the kind of love for him.

IX

There's something soldiers do on patrol - stop, take a look around and get acquainted with the environment – it's called a tactical pause. This is especially important at the beginning of a patrol. About thirty minutes into movement, the team stops, everyone faces out, takes a knee or gets into the prone for a few minutes to get accustomed to the sights, sounds and smells of the battlefield. And then periodically as the patrol makes movement it's a good idea to stop, do a map check, double check and confirm that you actually are where you think you are.

For Leon, Rudy's situation had reached the point for a tactical pause. He made a mental inventory.

This is what Leon knew, the 'knowns': Rudy killed Ivy, but Leon believed his story that it was self-defense. Then Rudy panicked and dumped her body in Drowning Creek, because he was obviously not thinking straight. If Rudy had been thinking straight, he wouldn't have dumped her there - not because Drowning Creek always gives up her dead – but because he had a pretty good case for self-defense and dumping the body did nothing but complicate the issue.

What else did he know? Leon knew that Gato was in town – a place where he certainly did not belong – that Ivy had been in touch with him, and that Gato was hanging out with a crew of mysterious Middle Easterners. Hispanic people are all over the place, of course, and so are people of Middle Eastern origin - this by itself means nothing. But this particular South

American happened to be a former Communist guerrilla with a history of engagement with U.S. Army Special Forces, and nobody in SF ever really liked the turd. For Gato to appear in the Fort Bragg area with a crew of geographically challenged foreigners got the hairs on the back of Leon's neck tingling. And when Ivy became aware that Rudy knew of her association with Gato & Co, this apparently drove her into a lethal rage, and this fact had Leon's Spidey Sense going off like red flags, bells, whistles, sirens, horns and klaxons all at the same time.

All the parts and pieces of a puzzle were there, but Leon did not know how they fit together. Then it occurred to him that perhaps all the pieces of the puzzle were not there. A few important pieces were missing. Who exactly were the Middle Eastern dudes, and what were they up to? Whatever it was, it could not be anything good. For Ivy to go off like she did, to try to kill her husband when she thought he was on to them, meant that whatever it was they were up to, it had to be bad.

And what about the Thing? The device he'd found in the locker out at the airport? It was important enough for Ivy to stash away from her husband, or anyone else. What did it mean, how did it tie in with everything else, if at all?

It was time to do a bit of snooping around. Leon had told C.I. everything he knew, and all he got back was to have faith, they'd be all over it. For Leon to go forth at this time as some sort of one-man investigation was against any and all operational principles, but Leon wasn't satisfied that those who were doing the investigation – if they were at all – shared his sense of urgency.

Surveillance is a team sport. Leon knew that to do a one-man surveillance on Gato and his crew was a bad plan because sooner or later they'd notice him, see a pattern, and then the danger is they'd go to ground, or worse, turn on Leon and try to eliminate him. Another problem with doing his own thing is the danger of parallel networks. This is when two 'friendly' intelligence organizations are operating within the same space, each without the knowledge of the other. There's a danger that when one of the organizations becomes aware of the other organizations' operations - not knowing who they are - the consequences can become very lethal, very quick.

Knowing all this, Leon decided that if he couldn't put effective surveillance on Gato and his band of merry men, then he'd set forth to seek out who was watching Gato, and he'd watch them. Like that old Elvis Costello song - 'Watching the Policemen'. This way he wasn't breaking the principles, not directly, anyway. Static surveillance was out of the question - Leon didn't have a place across the street to keep an eye on the target, and he didn't have a team to rotate in and out of position. Instead, he would make it a habit to drive past the house three times a day. To avoid drawing attention Leon would rotate out cars through a deal he cut with an ex-Special Forces buddy who ran a local rental car agency. Leon's buddy needed his cars washed, and Leon needed cars, so he washed them for free. No questions asked, and if there was going to be some action to get in on, he'd let him know.

It took Leon one rotation through Gato's street to make the surveillance team - two dickheads sitting right there on the side of the road in a white Chevy Impala. *'Are you kidding me?'* Leon thought. He was surprised they didn't have US Government plates on the damn thing. He rotated back two hours later, and they were still there. Leon looked around all over the place, maybe they were a decoy or something, but he couldn't loiter too long - the whole plan was to lay extremely low and just learn what he could. Watching the policemen.

Leon reckoned the worst thing he could do was become part of the clown show pulling surveillance on the house, so he decided it was time to drive up to Deep River Road and investigate the No-Name gas station that Rudy had told him about.

He knew where to go. Leon had been there before, but he'd never paid the place no mind - it just another run-down gas station of the type back when there were still mom & pop gas stations. A beat-up cinderblock building, two pumps, a small shop next to a small garage with three bays stuffed so full of old tires and crap there was barely enough room to work on one car. Grass was growing up through cracks in the paving, only one of the pumps worked and all they had was regular and premium, no mid-grade, super or anything exotic and of course no diesel, although they did have a sign saying they filled propane tanks and another pump off to the side marked 'Kerosene', and one of those air set ups you have to put quarters into to fill your tires. The place was tucked into the side of a hill overgrown with trees and scrub, so out of control it looked like the vegetation was in the process of devouring the hapless gas station.

Just as Leon was pulling in, he saw Gato coming out of the gas station's little convenience shop. Gato turned back to say something to someone inside, then continued walking to a gray green Subaru wagon. Leon slowed right down, pulled over to the air pump so he could get out without Gato seeing his face, and started messing with the air hose like he needed to fill his tires. Another individual emerged from the shop – tall, dark haired, bearded – and got into the passenger side of the Subaru.

Drowning Creek

Gato rolled out of there. Leon's plan was to let him clear the edge of the property, then hop back into his car and follow him at a distance. But just then two guys came out of the office and walked in his direction. Two Middle Eastern looking guys. Leon glanced up at them and continued with messing with the air pump and his tires.

One of the guys said something. Leon caught what he said - "*Bisho'ur.*" He was speaking Farsi. What he said: *idiot.*

The other guy replied. "*Dewane Sag.*" *Crazy dog.*

Leon got the impression they weren't speaking about each other, and himself being the only other person around, he had to hold back from blurting out, '*Khaar kosdeh.*' - *Your sister is a whore.* Leon understood this much Farsi. That narrowed down who they were and where they came from - Iranian.

Leon feigned ignorance as he finished up what he was doing, got into his truck and barreled down the road in search of Gato. He'd headed up Deep River Road to Highway 1 – but which way? North, or South? On a whim Leon took the entrance to Highway 1 North. It was worth breaking the speed limit - he figured he had maybe a fifty-fifty chance of catching up and finding Gato.

There's memory drill called Kim's Game. A box – like a cigar box or something – is opened and one looks at the items within for thirty seconds, before the lid is closed and then one is required to write them down, from memory. The name of the game comes from Rudyard Kipling's book 'Kim' - in British Colonial India, an orphaned street kid is trained as a spy by the British. A variant of the game is to walk into a room, have the briefest moment to flash on everything in the room, turn around and leave, then draw a diagram of the layout and contents of the room. Doing these drills helps one develop remarkable powers of perception and recall.

There were more than a few Subarus on the road. Leon reflected that the Raleigh-Durham-Chapel Hill area is literally infested with them. Leon had only had a fleeting glance at Gato's Subaru, but he caught up with him, unbelievably enough. It was easy to make him out - not only because Subarus stand out in general, but Gato's Subaru was the only one without a bunch of stickers like 'CO-EXIST' spelt out in different religious symbols, a peace symbol, or a rainbow decal in the back window. Leon was able to fade more than one vehicle back and still stay on Gato's tail.

Even still, surveillance is a team sport and by going it alone Leon was breaking every cardinal rule in the book. He was going to have to break it off, sooner or later. More sooner, than later. Leon figured he'd follow as long as it could reasonably be assumed he was just another vehicle going with the flow of traffic. When and if they got off the highway and went onto secondary roads or into a built-up urban area, it would be time to break it off.

Gato and his co-pilot continued up Highway 1 for about twenty minutes, taking the exit on I-440 / US-1 North, then merged onto I-40 West, towards Durham. This is still a main artery, so Leon kept following, hanging several vehicles back. About fifteen minutes down the road, they took the exit for Raleigh Road. A secondary road but still a two-lane highway. Nonetheless, in tailing them Leon had done three exits so far and so it was time to fade to gray.

Leon was looking around for a side street to turn onto as Raleigh Road narrowed into a regular urban road. A big sky-blue "Go Tarheels" painted on a building to his left informed him that he was now on the University of North Carolina campus, and just as he was looking for a direction to bug out, the big stadium loomed over to his ten o'clock. Leon now understood why Gato chose a Subaru – the place was absolutely infested with them. Still, Gato's Subaru stood out - no stickers.

Leon did one last glance just before he peeled off - Gato was gesturing towards the stadium. Something clicked in his mind for some odd reason, but he didn't know what it was, or why . . .

* * *

It was time for another tactical pause. Time for Leon to hold up, take a drink of water, look at the lay of the land, look where he was at and try to figure exactly what the hell was going on. He sure as hell couldn't think driving through all this city traffic. It was time to go home.

Leon took the long way back, down Highway 1 to Southern Pines, cut into the back side of Fort Bragg, down to Plank Road, then off the Fort Bragg reservation out to Raeford Road. It's a little longer, the better part of an hour, but there was no traffic to speak of, just long empty roads through mile after mile of pine trees and open fields. Just what he needed to get the creative juices going.

Once Leon hit Raeford Road it occurred to him that he was closer to Rudy's place than to his own. Maybe if he revisited the scene of the crime, sat inside Rudy's house and looked around, something might get jarred loose inside his brain to make some kind of sense of the whole thing, whatever that might be.

'Connect the dots,' he thought. *'I need to connect the dots.'* But in order to do this, Leon needed to know what the dots were. When he got to Rudy's place, he pulled into the driveway and sat there for a few minutes, to see if the place was being watched – from the street at least – and to let the neighborhood watch see that he's not some kind of Fayetteville punk, come to ransack the place. When he went in, this time he closed the front door. This way, if the guy from next door showed up, at least Leon would hear him coming.

Leon went back to Rudy's office, looked at the pictures of him and Ivy. Again, that kind of creepy feeling. He located a large yellow legal pad and a pen in one of Rudy's desk drawers, put it down on the desk and started making a list of everything he knew to date.

One. Ivy was hanging out with Gato and his sinister Middle Eastern crew.

Two. When Ivy became aware that Rudy knew about it, had her under surveillance, she went ballistic and came at him with her straight razor - ergo . . .

Three. Ivy had something serious going on with Gato. Something damn serious. Serious enough to kill over.

Four. What is the meaning of that weird device, that Ivy had stashed in the airport rental locker? How does it tie in, if at all?

Five. Gato and his weird crew hang out at the No-Name gas station on Deep River Road.

Six. Gato and one of his cohorts went for a drive today, up to Chapel Hill.

Drowning Creek

'*What's in Chapel Hill that may be significant?*' Leon asked himself. If this is one of the dots, how does it connect? What were they doing, a drug run? Leon wouldn't put it past Gato to be dealing drugs. A guy's gotta make a living, right? Leon closed his eyes and tried to revisit what was going on the last few blocks he followed Gato, before breaking contact.

The stadium. Gato was gesturing towards the stadium – so Leon wrote that down -

Seven. Stadium, UNC.

What possible significance could the stadium have? Leon pulled out his phone and looked up stadium, UNC -

> *Kenan Memorial Stadium is located in Chapel Hill, North Carolina and is the home field of the North Carolina Tar Heels. It is primarily used for football. The stadium opened in 1927 and holds 50,500 people. It is located near the center of campus at the University of North Carolina.*

Fifty thousand people. Leon supposed that was pretty big for a college football stadium built in the twenties. Maybe if he threw some analysis on it, something would come up. So he looked up the two other stadiums in the vicinity - Duke, Wake Forest.

Wallace Wade Stadium is the stadium for Duke University in Durham. Forty thousand seat capacity. Truist Field is the home field for Wake Forest, capacity thirty-one thousand people.

'Okay,' Leon thought, '*So UNC is the big one. So what? What's the big deal about a football stadium?*' Then he thought, '*I gotta put myself inside the head of the enemy.*'

'*Okay,*' he thought again, '*If I was a bad guy, and I wanted to do something totally evil, a football stadium is a good place to fuck up a lot of people.*'

Then it came to him, a total revelation. It went off in Leon's head like a flash – something Rudy had said:

> *"I was up in Raleigh, part of this project I was on. We want to bring the Army-Navy game down to Raleigh-Durham area. You know it's always up by DC, or around Annapolis, or Philly, or New York. Well, a bunch of us officers who graduated from UNC and Duke and Wake Forest wanted to bring the game down here, and I was point man in trying to arrange things."*

'*The fucking Army-Navy game!*' Leon did another search on his phone and sure enough -

> *The Army-Navy game is scheduled to be played this year at Kenan Memorial Stadium in Chapel Hill, North Carolina.*

Leon didn't think he'd connected the dots, just yet, but maybe he was beginning to find out what the dots actually were.

X

Leon kicked back and put his thinking bone on it, tried to put himself right inside the head of his enemy. '*If I was a bad guy,*' he figured, '*and I wanted to fuck up a whole bunch of people, do a significant terrorist attack, taking out the combined West Point Corps of Cadets and the U.S. Naval Academy Brigade of Midshipmen would put a giant hole in the leadership of the U.S. military and would definitely put me right up there in the same league as Osama bin Laden.*'

Ok, so now Leon had the Who and the What, the Where and the When. All he needed to figure was the How, or How Many, to make his theory turn into a viable hypothesis.

Just then he heard the door opening. Leon glanced out the office door into the living room. It was Special Agent Johnson, the CID guy.

"What the fuck are you doing here, Leon? Didn't you see the yellow crime tape?"

"Yeah, fuck that shit. Sit down, I've got something to tell you."

Nobody talks to a CID investigator like that. Well, Leon just did. Johnson gave him an odd look, then he pulled up a chair and sat down.

Leon told him what he knew and what he'd seen. He didn't get to the part about the stadium yet, or his conclusions. Johnson was looking at him with this fucked up look on his face.

"Let me see if I'm hearing this right. You went to where these guys are, encountered them up close and personal, then followed two of them down the road? You mean to tell me you're actually pulling one-man surveillance on these guys? You realize you're breaking every rule in the book, right? This is a totally amateur move. You know this, right? It's possible you have endangered any actual legitimate surveillance there is on these guys. You know this, right?"

"Hold on," Leon said, "I didn't exactly pull surveillance, and yes, I understand it takes three or more teams to pull mobile surveillance. I just went down the highway same direction they were going to where the highway became a road with traffic lights and intersections, and I pulled off as soon as they got into a built-up area. The built-up area just so happened to be the UNC campus, Chapel Hill."

"So?"

"Last thing I saw, just before I took the nearest right turn away from them, was Gato gesturing to the UNC stadium, telling his sidekick some shit."

"So?"

"So, nothing. He's gesturing towards a stadium. No law against that, right?"

"Right."

"So, I'm sitting here trying to make sense of everything, trying to find a common thread. I wrote everything down so I could see all the moving parts . . ."

"If there are any moving parts," Johnson interrupted.

"Uh, yeah," Leon said. Then he showed Johnson his notes. "These are our knowns: first of all, Haglin strangles Ivy, and he's claiming self-defense, says she came at him with a straight razor after she discovers he's had her followed and has pics of her hanging out at Gato's place, with the weird Middle Easterners."

"Right."

"So something's going on with Gato and his crew. Something so hot and intense enough to drive Ivy to want to kill."

"Possibly."

"Possibly," Leon acknowledged. He didn't tell Johnson about the device he'd found in the locker at the airport. He was holding that close for now, until he knew what it was and if it meant anything at all. "If Haglin's telling the truth – and I believe he is, and in my opinion the cuts all over his forearms backstop this – then there's something going on with Gato. The guy is up to no good, and Ivy was somehow involved. She wasn't just hanging out with Gato and company so they could pull trains on her."

Johnson winced at the thought of this.

"So now Gato is possibly interested in something up in Chapel Hill, and that something might be the football stadium."

"That's a couple of maybes right there," Johnson pointed out. "What's the significance of the football stadium?"

"Nothing, it's just a football stadium," Leon replied, and Johnson gave him that deadpan look again. "Except for the fact that the Army-Navy game is scheduled to be played there this year. In a couple weeks, in fact."

The look on Johnson's face went from deadpan to dead serious.

"Haglin was directly involved in getting the game to be played down here in North Carolina, apparently. And that puts Ivy right in the middle of all these moving parts." I pointed to my list on the yellow legal pad. "All these parts and pieces suddenly mesh and are turning around like a set of gears in one great big fucking machine."

Johnson looked at Leon's list, looked up at Leon, looked down again at the list, and then looked back up at Leon again. Johnson was seeing it.

"You've got the Who, What, Where, and When right there."

"I know," Leon said.

"All you're missing is the How."

"All YOU'RE missing is the How," Leon said. "I'm not a part of this thing. I'm not an investigator – you said so yourself."

"This thing we're looking at here isn't even a crime yet," Johnson said. "It's a theory of yours."

"A hypothesis," Leon said, "which is a theory on steroids."

"Okay, but if there's a crime here," Johnson went on, "or rather, a crime in the making, then two things - it's going to be pretty damn big . . ."

"Huge," Leon said.

"Yeah, huge," Johnson went on, "and it's above and beyond the scope of the CID. We'd be remiss if we didn't get counterintelligence in on this."

"That's exactly what I was thinking."

"The U.S. Army Criminal Investigation Division is responsible for conducting felony-level criminal investigations in which the Army is, or may be, a party of interest."

"Right."

"That's a pretty wide scope of interest – we're basically the Army's police department."

"Right."

"The Counter-Intelligence Command is charged with investigation of five crimes - treason, sedition, espionage, subversion, and sabotage."

"Right," Leon said again. "I think a possible terrorist plot by international bad guys falls in there somewhere. I think we've got all of them in here except maybe treason. If Ivy was alive, we'd have that even."

"Except she's dead, so there's no crime there, anymore."

"Maybe," Leon said. "She's dead, but that doesn't mean she didn't do the crime, it just means there's no prosecution for a crime that happened. Anyway, four out of five ain't bad."

"Yeah," Roberts said. "We need to get the FBI in on this shit, too."

"Absolutely. And we need to figure out how to tell those guys without us coming across sounding like a pair of loons."

XI

Leon went home. He was tempted to go to the bar, to see what was going on with Jill and Nancy - it had been a long day in an already too long week – but it wasn't Monday and he really couldn't deal with the thought of a crowded bar. He needed to relax.

His phone rang.

"Hey." A woman's voice.

"Hey, yerself."

"It's Nancy."

"Yes."

"I wanted to know if you're interested in doing something."

'*This is interesting*,' Leon thought. There once was a time he couldn't get a date in this town. Now, the dates were coming to him. He supposed this was a measure of success.

"Sure," he said, "but aren't you dancing?"

"It's Thursday," she said. "Thursdays are my night off."

"Okay," he said. "Then what do you want to do? You want to go out to dinner, or would you prefer a home cooked meal?"

"Oh my God," she said, "I live in a hotel room and I eat in restaurants every day. A home cooked meal sounds like heaven!"

Drowning Creek

"You want me to swing by and pick you up?"

"Could you?"

She told him the place - a cheap ass hotel down on Bragg Boulevard where the stripper bar circuit parks their girls. Leon tried to imagine how it must be for these girls, such a lonely life. Then again, he figured, most people don't know how Green Berets do it. A person can adapt to almost anything, he supposed. Then Leon thought of Rudy, cooling his heels in the brig. He hoped Rudy's spirits were holding up. He'd have to tool over there and let Rudy know his progress. Maybe talk with Rudy's lawyer, compare notes.

Nancy looked like Cleopatra, walking out of that dump. Some women have got it, can look like a beauty queen no matter where they are, even if she's wearing only a potato sack – Nancy was one of them, apparently.

The only other time he'd seen her at a distance was when she was writhing around the pole on stage half-naked, then later in her string-kini, walking towards him and sitting next to him at the bar. This evening she wore tight jeans, a short bunny jacket over a top that featured a very interesting neckline and a black leather choker. Leon's jaw dropped. Stunning brunette.

Leon got out of his car and opened the door for Nancy. It's something Leon's generation did but judging by the look of pleasant surprise on her face, it's something different for her generation. Then he walked back around to his side, got in and it was Leon's turn for a pleasant surprise when she landed a big wet one right on the lips.

"That was nice," he said, putting his arm across her shoulders.

"It's nice of you to pick me up."

"Yeah, well, taxis are a roll of the dice in this town."

"It's nice to get out of that place," she indicated the hotel with a nod of her head. "It's nice to have a night out for a change."

"If you want to go out, we can go and do something. A movie, or . . ." Leon was about to say dancing, but he caught himself. *'What exactly does a dancer do on her day off?'*

"Nah. I'd rather stick with the plan. Your place. We can, you know, Netflix and chill."

Leon smiled. *'With these gigantic flatscreens everyone has nowadays, does anybody even go to the movies anymore?'* In Leon's opinion, it's not as if they're making movies that are actually even worth watching any more.

When they got to his place, Leon backed into his garage. "Why do you guys always do this?" she asked.

"Do what?"

"Park backwards like that."

"It only makes sense," he said.

"What do you mean?"

"Right now, I've got all the time in the world to park," Leon said. "But I might have to get out of here in a hurry. You never know."

"It must be a military thing. My Dad always parks like that." Then she looked at Leon and smiled – it was a smile that said so much. Leon smiled back, because he caught the unspoken message: *You're old enough to be my Dad.*

"Your dad's in the service?"

"He was. He was a SEAL."

"Really? Where are you from?"

"Florida."

"What part?"

"Melbourne."

"I've been there. Nice part of Florida."

The garage opened into the kitchen. He walked her through to the living room, put on the music channel. "What kind of music do you like?"

"Blues," she said. "I like the blues." Leon was liking the girl more and more every minute. Leon went to the music channels and clicked on Deep Blues. Nancy started swaying her body to the rhythm, writhing like when he'd first laid eyes on her. Leon smiled - she sure could move her curves. The song went into a saxophone solo and it was like the night he met her, only then she was naked and right now her clothes were on. It didn't matter somehow - even fully dressed, Nancy was sexy as hell.

"I love the blues," she said. "My girlfriend and I were driving up here from Florida, and we hit this place in Georgia. How the hell we found it I don't know, we were on the back roads. There was this black man in there playing the guitar, and he was playing blues tunes, and it was so beautiful, the music he was playing, the blues he was playing was so deep and so beautiful you just wanted to cry."

"I love the blues," Leon said.

"Yeah," she said.

Nancy looked at the stuff Leon had up on the walls – some artifacts he'd picked up in the Middle East, in a corner the usual team photos, the obligatory hero photo of himself brandishing an AK, a few old plaques, his decorations. She pointed at a picture he'd taken in the Old City, Jerusalem. "You've been to Israel?"

"Twice."

"Oh . . ." she sighed. "Did you have an Israeli girlfriend when you were there?"

"I did, actually, for a while," he said. Then he added, wistfully, "That was a long time ago,"

"Tell me about Israel," she said.

"Well, Eilat and Tel Aviv are party towns, and the girls are really friendly, and they hang out at the beach in their bikinis with their rifles slung across their bodies like a girl carries a bag, over here. Sometimes topless."

"They really do that?"

"They really do that. When they're on active duty – you know, they're in the Army reserves all their life – they have to carry their weapon with them everywhere they go. Also, I guess it's part of the security situation."

"And in Jerusalem?"

"It's a completely different scene. Jerusalem isn't a party town. An Israeli girl won't have anything to do with an American guy in Jerusalem, not unless she's married or engaged to him. The rules are completely different."

"Huh."

"Yeah. You know, the Temple, and all that."

"You've been to the Temple Mount?"

"Yes."

"You've been to the Kotel? The Wall?"

"Yes."

"Are you Jewish?"

"No," he said. Then, on a whim, "Why do you ask? Are you Jewish?"

"I am."

Leon smiled wide. There's something about sexy Jewish girls.

"You ever married?" she asked.

"No," he said.

"Why not?"

"Well, nearly, once," he said, wistfully. "But it didn't work out. Work kept me busy. The Forever War."

"The Israeli girl?"

"No. English girl, actually."

"Oh." Nancy sensed a poignant memory. Then, "Got any kids?"

"None that I know of," he said, "but if you're interested, maybe we could try and . . ."

"Oh no!" she laughed. Leon didn't add that if he did have any kids, they'd be her age.

Leon looked at Nancy, she was still swaying to the music, doing her dancer's moves. The girl had a body that wouldn't quit, and she knew how to move it - slim, full, round breasts and a nice, long pair of legs. Leon moved close to dance with her, put his hand on the small of her back, pressed his body to hers and they swayed together. They danced slow, real slow. Then they stopped dancing and they kissed. When they finally broke the kiss Nancy murmured, "Please," with tremble in her voice that sounded like she was begging for it, "Make love to me?" It was time to move it to the bedroom.

Sex with Nancy was like driving a powerful Italian sports car. First the incredible beauty of the machine takes your breath away – the curves, the symmetry of design so pleasing to the eye. Then you step into the car and the luxurious interior, the exquisite upholstery - soft but firm - adds touch to the sensory experience. Then you engage the ignition, fire up the motor and take her to the road and everything you give to her she bounces right back, wrapping around tight curves with a sensation of total control, even at top speeds. The powerful engine surges forward, you ride on suspension that feels like you're floating on air, a machine so smooth you feel like you're practically standing still while you're zooming down the highway, no speed limit.

Leon marveled as Nancy rode him, taking her pleasure with confidence and skill. Then they rotated and the power exchange switched, and he was giving it to her like a marauding warrior. She clutched at him, holding on for dear life as he pressed forward in the advance, showing no quarter until the hill was crested, the battle gained, and they reached a higher level where they were naught but two souls - out of body, out of mind - all sensations and consciousness reduced to the purest joy and pleasure that a man and a woman can experience this side of Paradise.

He'd spent the last twenty years as a modern-day Viking - now in Nancy he'd finally met a Valkyrie who was taking him by the hand, embracing him and carrying him on an ascent up to Asgard, Home of the Viking Gods.

Afterwards, as they lay back recovering their senses, she asked, "Penny for your thoughts?"

"I dunno. There's a lot going on. There's this thing I'm getting involved in, which I don't want to be involved in. A friend – a good friend – is in a lot of trouble, and I'm trying to get him out of it. It's not as if anyone's on vacation right now, around here."

"I get it," Nancy said. "There's work to do. A lot of work." She leaned over and kissed him on the cheek. "But for now, this is a vacation, this is a break."

Leon sensed what she was talking about, but she was right - there was no way he could have possibly imagined how crazy things were going to get, and how incredibly busy he was going to be working it.

Then she got up and did her little run to the bathroom, and then Leon did his run to the bathroom.

Afterwards, laying together in bed, Nancy studied Leon's face. "How old are you?" she asked.

"Forty."

"You don't look it. You look like you're thirty. Thirty-five, at the most."

"Yeah, well, all that good living, I guess." Then, "I've been on the Olympic Team for twenty years."

"What do you mean?"

"I'm in the part of the Army where they put all the crazy people."

"Ha! What do you mean by that?"

"I'm a Green Beret."

"Oh, I get it," she said. "Like my Dad."

"Yes. Sort of like your Dad."

"You know, you're old enough to be my Dad."

"I wasn't going to say anything." What a conversation killer.

It was early still, especially for a stripper. Those girls pull late hours and there was still a lot of evening to go. "Let's get in the shower," Leon suggested.

"Let's," she agreed. "Sex always makes you feel like a glazed doughnut."

That made him laugh.

"Well, it does!"

Showering with a friend is what it's all about, the slippery feeling, rubbing two soaped-up bodies together. Nancy had a body that was totally pneumatic, round in all the right places, bouncy yet firm, well-rounded hips to hold on to while he rubbed himself all over her. They got it started in the shower, then moved it back into the bedroom for Round Two. The woman had a libido that wouldn't quit.

Being in bed with Nancy was lovemaking on a whole other level. Leon hated to admit it, but they obviously clicked. Sex with Nancy more intimate, romantic - even spiritual – and it scared him to death. There was intense eye contact, a lot of kissing before, during, throughout. They took their time, every move was special as they pleasured one another. Their bodies fitting perfectly to one another, legs intertwined, until they were just two souls clinging to one another until they traveled to the outskirts of Heaven and returned.

Then afterwards they held each other close, and Leon was gentle and affectionate as he touched her, his hand on her cheek, kissing her face, her neck, her breasts.

Leon got up early the next morning, before six. Years of habit. Strippers sleep in till about one in the afternoon, which makes sense, considering their hours.

* * *

Leon got word from Rudy's lawyer - they were cutting Rudy loose on bail, so he and the lawyer met up and drove over to Lejeune to pick him up. Rudy was pale and his face was puffy. Not much was said while the Marines processed him out of the brig. Once outside, Rudy turned to Leon.

"Thanks, Leon." He was squinting in the sunlight.

"No problem, sir – you'd have done the same thing for me." When they got in Leon's truck, Leon handed him a beer.

"Uh, that's illegal," the lawyer said.

"Only if you're caught," Leon said.

"What I mean is, at least wait until you get off post," the lawyer said.

"Uh, hold the can down until I get us past the gate, sir," Leon said to Rudy, acknowledging the lawyer's guidance. Once they were off post and heading down the main road back to Bragg, Leon spoke up. "Listen, sir, I don't think it's a good idea you stay at your place."

"Why not?"

"Think about it. Whatever drove Ivy to try to wipe you out has got something to do with Gato and his crew, and they know your place."

"Hmmm."

"According to the conditions of his parole, Lieutenant-Colonel Haglin is confined to quarters," the lawyer spoke up. "That means he has to be at his place of residence."

"Don't fuckin' worry about it," Leon said. "For now, my place is his place of residence, we'll put him on my recognizance."

"I must strongly advise you," the lawyer spoke up again, "Lieutenant-Colonel Haglin is confined to quarters, and if he's anywhere but at his place of residence, this will invalidate his parole, will send him right back into incarceration and will have an extremely negative effect on his case. The court may choose to view it like he's attempting to influence the case, witness tampering, etcetera."

"Shit," Leon muttered. "I don't like it."

"It is what it is," Rudy said quietly. "I'll be okay."

"I'm gonna swing past my place so I can give you one of my guns," Leon said.

"You certainly can't do that," the lawyer protested.

Drowning Creek

"Why the fuck not? He's charged, he ain't convicted of anything. We still have a Second Amendment in this country. Hell, a Fourth Amendment, too." Leon went on. "If Gato's crew is watching the place, they'll know he's back in town and we don't want that."

"We can pull into a shopping center – I don't think they've got any malls out here in the boondocks – get you some gear."

"Well, we can have the CID guys talk to the MPs, have them show up at the place," the lawyer said, "make a visible presence, maybe roll by on a regular courtesy patrol."

"Okay, I guess that'll have to work," Leon said. He didn't like it, but it was what it was.

When they got to Fayetteville, Leon swung by the lawyer's offices and dropped him off, then brought Rudy to his place. Leon asked to use the bathroom, then was about to leave, let Rudy relax.

When Leon came back into the living room, Rudy walked in from his little office room. "What happened to my papers, my laptop, all that stuff?"

"You're going to have to make do without," Leon said. "There's an ongoing investigation, any and all of that is now evidence. They seized everything. Right now you don't even have a phone. As far as the internet goes, I suggest you avoid all of your social media, email even. You don't need to be leaving any kind of digital trail," Leo advised.

"Shit."

"Yeah. You're in a world of shit right now, but it could be worse."

"What do you mean?"

"You could be dead, sir," Leon said. "That is an actual option, and that's why I'm handing over my piece." Leon drew his 1911, dropped the magazine, cleared the pistol and locked the slide to the rear, and handed it over to Rudy. Then he handed over the magazine, the extra round that had been in the chamber, and the two extra mags he always carried in his pockets.

"Wow," Rudy said, "You carry the Big Boy, the forty-five."

"Yessir," Leon replied. "Sure do."

"Why don't you like the nine mil? There's more rounds in a fifteen-round mag, than in a seven-round."

"It's not that I have anything against nine millimeter," Leon answered, "But if I need fifteen rounds to do what I gotta do, then I'm in the wrong movie. End of the day, my handgun is only for fighting my way back to my truck gun."

Rudy shrugged.

"I'm going to the store to get some groceries, some bread and fixin's so you can make yourself a sandwich, something like that," Leon said, "If you like, I can swing by my place and bring you back a nine mill. I actually own a Glock, and I own a CZ-75. Which would you prefer?"

"Either, or," Rudy said.

"Fine," said Leon. "I'll give you the Glock – it's a war souvenir, it's numbers aren't on anybody's list, anywhere past the factory."

"Thank you," Leon replied. Then, "You know, since we're involved in this thing, so close like this, it's kind of weird for you having to call me 'sir' all the time. You might as well call me Rudy."

"I don't want to cross that line of familiarity," Leon said. "We're both still in the Army – at least for now - and you're still an officer."

"Well, you're, what, retiring next month, is it? That means you're practically a civilian."

"That's true," Leon acknowledged.

"Tell you what," Rudy said, "You can call me by my code name."

"We always did, Shitbags," Leon grinned.

"That's not my code name!" Rudy protested. Then, "Is it?"

"No, I was just fucking with you," Leon grinned even wider, and Rudy was grinning, too. "Rudy it is, then," he said. It was a necessary ice breaker.

* * *

Later, back at his place, Leon was shaving while Nancy pulled on some clothes. When Leon walked into the living room. Nancy was perusing his bookshelf, had a book out.

"What have you got there?" She showed him - *Atlas Shrugged*, by Ayn Rand. Leon arched an eyebrow.

"Can I borrow this?"

"Sure," Leon said. "Ayn Rand is some pretty deep stuff. It's a hefty read."

"You mean, some pretty deep stuff for a stripper to be reading."

"No, I meant exactly what I said. It takes some time to plow through, and it was written over sixty years ago. You have to be pretty well informed just to look it up. Are you familiar with her works?""

"Yes, actually. Just because I'm a dancer doesn't mean I'm stupid."

"No, of course not. When you actually think about it, within the club environment, the dancers hold the intellectual high ground."

"What do you mean?"

"Well, the guys throwing the dollar bills at the girls aren't exactly Nobel Prize winners."

"I've read her other two books. The concepts she presents are profound, they really apply to a lot of what's going on out there these days. I think everyone should read Ayn Rand."

"Tell you what," Leon said. "You can take it with you, it's an old copy. Or you can leave it here, and read it when you're here."

"Am I going to be here long enough to read all of this?" She held up the book. Atlas Shrugged is as thick as a phone book.

"Why not? You got someplace better to be?"

"The hotel sucks. I'd give anything to get out of there."

"You can hang out here," Leon said. "I like having somebody around the house, actually." Right about now every alarm bell in Leon's head was going off and he couldn't believe what he'd just blurted out.

"Are you serious?"

"We can see how it goes," he shrugged.

"God, I'd do anything to get out of that hotel."

"Anything?"

"Ha ha. Well, maybe not anything, but a lot. You know what I mean." She winked, and Leon grinned back.

* * *

Early Saturday morning, Nancy looked a bit tired when Leon picked her up. They went to her hotel to pick up her things. First order of business was a shower. Leon was going to give her some distance, she'd just got off work, but Nancy called him into the bathroom. "You're not going to join me?"

Leon shrugged off his gear and joined her in the shower. He ran his hands all over her. Later, drying her off with a big fluffy hotel towel, Leon asked "You're not sick of guys, at the end of a shift?"

"No, not really. Doing all those lap dances actually, well, hard to say it. Puts me into a sort of heightened state."

"Hmmm. I often wondered about that." She grabbed him. "Wow," Leon said, "you're ready for that?"

"Yeah."

"I thought maybe you wanted to go out, get a bite to eat."

"I'll eat you and you eat me. Food, later."

"Don't you want to get the hell out of this hotel, and we can do it at my place?"

"Hmmm. Yeah. Good idea. More better, there."

"Anyway we can eat at my place, too. Better than a greasy spoon diner, which is all that's open this time of night, anyway."

Later on, pillow talk - "You said anything," he said.

"Anything," she replied. "Well, within reason."

"I want to play Twenty Questions."

"Okay, that's reasonable. Almost, I guess."

"You're like what, twenty?"

"Twenty-four, actually."

"When did you ever find time to read Ayn Rand's first two books?"

"A lot of long, boring hours during the day. You can only do so many hours in the gym, you know. And it helps to put something up there on the walker when you're getting in your miles."

"Must've put in a lot of miles going through those books. No wonder you've got such a tight ass."

"Ha ha." Then, "What do you do in the Army?"

"Nothing much. I'm getting ready to drop my retirement paperwork. Nowadays I just ride herd on a bunch of trainees. Show them how to do Army stuff, tricks of the trade, how not to get kicked out of the Q Course."

Drowning Creek

"What's the Q Course?"

"The Special Forces Qualification Course."

"Is that what you are? Special Forces?"

"Yes, I'm a Green Beret."

"My Dad is a SEAL."

"Yes, you told me, before."

"My Dad was in the Gulf War. The first one - Desert Storm. Were you there?"

"No, I was in the Philippines at that time."

"Oh, that sounds nice."

"It was, actually. Both sides always run out of ammo early in the fight, then they both go home."

"Is that why you're so laid back? My Dad is wound up tight, like a clock spring, and he goes off at the smallest thing."

"No. I guess I'm laid back because I learned early on that holding on to anger is like drinking poison and expecting the other person to die."

"What are you angry about?"

"What is there not to be angry about? The world is turning to shit more and more every day, and it's almost as if it's by design, by the powers-that-be."

"Who is John Galt?" Nancy quoted.

"Exactly . . ."

Peter Crittenden

* * *

Leon was having his morning cup of coffee when suddenly there was a loud noise out in front of his place. He glanced through the glass panes on the sides of his door and saw a blue Dodge Challenger pull onto his front yard, right across his lawn, diagonal. '*What the fuck,*' he thought.

He retrieved his downstairs .45 from where he kept it in the liquor cabinet, slapped in a mag, smacked the bottom of the magazine to click it home, and jacked a round in the chamber. Then he cracked open his front door to deal with this latest challenge. The car door opened and this reprobate emerged, a half Hispanic, half black looking guy in a Dallas Cowboys jersey and a loose pair of pants that hung down his ass, the way the shitheads like to wear them.

"Where's Torres?" he asked.

"Ain't no Torres here," Leon said.

Shithead got back in his car, appeared to make or take a phone call, then suddenly he opened the door, produced what looked like a Glock and fired at Leon. The shithead missed Leon, but not by much. Leon pulled back trying to make himself as slim as possible behind the door frame – the only cover available – as he fired back. Leon fired three more times and watched bullet holes spider out the laminated glass in the rear window of the car. He was pretty sure he also put one in the back of the trunk as Shithead sped off down the street.

Leon glanced up and down the street, then closed the door, unloaded and cleared his pistol. His hands were shaking slightly from the adrenalin that was still coursing through his veins. He looked up.

Drowning Creek

...y was standing in the bedroom doorway, wrapped in a ...eet, looking at him with wide eyes. "What's going on?"

"I'm not sure. Some scumbag rolled up on the lawn, got out of his car, asked if a guy called Rudy was here, then started shooting at me, so I shot back."

"Holy shit! Does that kind of thing happen very often around here?"

"Not exactly, but sometimes shit happens. I'm going to have to fix the door." The door had three bullet holes in it. Then Leon and Nancy both looked at the wall opposite the front door. There were three bullet holes in the sheet rock. "And the wall, I guess," he added. "You want a cup of coffee?"

"I'd really rather go back to bed, but there's no way I could get back to sleep now, after this, so yeah, I guess coffee would be nice."

Leon called the Cumberland County Sheriff's Department. When the deputies showed up, he told them what happened.

The deputies already knew Leon - he'd been to court twice in Fayetteville for standing up against drug dealers. The way Leon saw it, there's only one way to play it - set the momentum and the pace and don't let them get any traction. He'd even heard about the drug dealers calling the police in tears.

Leon had done it alone, but it damn near broke him psychologically.

The neighbors - some Special Forces guys, some 82nd Infantry, some MPs even - were afraid. Many asked Leon to report third hand information. Many talked about guns, having guns, and how they would take care of criminals, but there's a big difference between talk and having the balls to actually do anything about it. Many tucked in their tails when the low riders rolled up in front of their houses, brazenly dealing drugs in the street, only to come out talking smack when the coast was clear. All talk.

The way Leon saw it, the only thing criminals respect is violence, and the police are always late. They will not sit in your yard to prevent an attack.

"Why'd he open fire on you?"

"All I can think is it was a case of mistaken identity, the shithead had the wrong address. As you should already be aware, a couple of my neighbors up the street have a long history for drug sales."

Leon had caught this morning's event on video – he had four high quality cameras up, and after this morning he was thinking about adding another four to cover the entire property.

"Would you mind if we run a K9 through your house?"

"W-H-A-A-A-?-?-?"

"Well, we've got an exchange of gunfire on your property and it looks like its drug related. We have to do it, it's part of the investigation. We could get a warrant - there's reasonable cause – or if you give us the OK we can have the dog over here in less than thirty minutes, run him through your place and then we're out of here."

"Okay, you can bring the damn dog in," Leon said. "But let me talk to my girlfriend – she was in bed asleep when this whole thing happened, let me at least make sure she's decent."

Drowning Creek

"Yes sir, go ahead."

Nancy was sitting at the table, looking at her phone.

"Check it out, the sheriff's deputies are bringing a dog in to sniff the place for drugs. Do you have anything on you?"

"W-h-a-a-a-?"

"Yeah," Leo said, "this thing was possibly drug related, so they want to clear me out as part of their investigation. Now, do you have anything on you, anything at all? Any blow? A roach, even?"

"No. If I did, I would have used it last night, wouldn't I? But I don't. I don't have any grass, I don't have any coke. I don't even like coke, it makes me bitchy."

"Are you sure?"

"Sure, I'm sure."

"I'm going to ask you one last time, if you have anything on you – anything stronger than an aspirin – flush it down the toilet. Please."

"Are you saying you don't believe me?"

"I don't believe anything anyone says anymore, don't take it personal," Leo said. "Look – I'll make it worth your while." He got out his wallet and handed her a couple of hundreds. "If you've got anything on you, flush it down the toilet, then go buy yourself more, later."

"Not all dancers use drugs, you know."

What Leon left unsaid was, *'Not all dancers are pros,'* as Nancy quietly pocketed the bills. This didn't bother Leon, he liked to know the limits.

"I hope you're being straight with me Nancy, because my career won't be able to stand it if Fido alerts on anything in your bag."

They brought the dog in. The dog sniffed around, found nothing. Nancy glared at Leon.

"Now go catch his ass," Leon said to the deputy. "Shouldn't be too hard – how many blue Challengers are there driving around here with three bullet holes in the rear window? Plus, we've got the whole thing on video – probably got the plates, even."

'The best thing would be is to move,' Leon thought. A guy can fight, and a guy can win in a gunfight, but no amount of money or gunslinging is worth the trouble. Life is precious. *'They don't call this place FayetteNam for nothing.'*

XII

The business with the sheriff's deputy and the dog concluded, Leon went back inside. Nancy was sitting on the edge of the bed, holding her phone. She looked up at Rudy.

"You hurt me."

'*What now,*' he thought.

"What am I," she asked, "your whore girlfriend?"

"I didn't realize we were at the boyfriend-girlfriend stage," Leon answered.

Nancy's reply was a look of shock and outrage - like, "Did you just call me a whore? No, wait a minute – I called myself a whore. No, wait a minute . . ."

"Sorry, hon, I didn't mean it that way," Leon caught himself. "But hell, if you fling any of that female verbal jiu-jitsu at me, I'm just going to fling it right back, that's the way I roll. There's no way I'm going to get sucked into mind games."

Leon noticed she'd tucked away the two hundred dollars, so he guessed she wasn't that hurt.

He went on. "Nothing personal, but I just had at least six bullets launched at me at point blank range, and then the cops wanted to send a K9 through here. My nerves were a little on edge and I had to deal with the situation. Thank you, by the way, for not being a doper. That actually means a lot to me."

"I'm a dancer, but I'm not stupid. Everything's mixed with fentanyl these days, even grass. Girls who do lines, girls who drop what they think is Ecstasy, girls who toke up, they're O.D.-ing, dropping like flies."

There was a brief pause. Then Leon said, "I'm grateful you're not a user. I really am. You don't know how much I am." He leaned forward and gently kissed Nancy on the forehead. "Let me make it up to you."

"How?"

"I dunno," Leon said. Then, "I know, how would you like to get out of town? A little vacation."

"Where?"

"Let's go to the beach."

"The beach? This time of year?"

"Yeah! The Carolina coast is fantastic, the beaches are amazing, especially this time of year when there's nobody there. It's not hot and warm but it's really not that cold. We'll have the entire place to ourselves and it's so relaxing to walk up and down the beach."

"That actually sounds pretty cool."

"Yeah," Leon went on. "You know, long relaxing walks on the beach. Just like they write in the lonely-hearts ads."

Nancy's face brightened up. "Let's do it, Leon."

"I've got a friend who's got one of those beach houses, it's like two houses, one up on top of the other, up on stilts. He always lets me stay there, any time I want. This time of year we'll have the place to ourselves, we'll have the whole beach to ourselves."

"That sounds great, Leon," Nancy said. "Let's do it. Can we swing by the hotel so I can grab some things?"

"Yes, of course."

"And I'd like a quick shower before we take off, is that OK?"

"Yes, I need a shower myself. We'll save time if we . . ."

Nancy laughed at this. "Take more time, is more like it."

* * *

There wasn't much to pack, they wouldn't be swimming or socializing. One thing Leon did grab was The Thing – the strange cylindrical object he'd recovered from the airport locker, using the key he'd found in Ivy's handbag. Looking at the strange thing with its smooth metallic surface, inscriptions and crystalline panels, Leon wondered if it emitted any kind of passive signal, like the way a smartphone can be tracked even if you've got the location services and GPS turned off. While Nancy was getting ready, Loen put the device back into the manila envelope, then went into the kitchen and retrieved the aluminum foil. He wrapped aluminum foil around the manila envelope five times, folded the edges on both ends, creating a crude but hopefully effective Faraday bag. Then he deposited the entire affair in a brown paper shopping bag, folded it neatly into a flat square and taped it shut.

Nancy threw her toothbrush and some things into a bag and then they were on the road to the coast. They stopped in the town of Duck to pick up some food and drink. Nancy was curious why Leon purchased a frozen turkey.

"It'll be Thanksgiving soon," he said. "If we come back to the beach house, this way we'll have a turkey."

Nancy shrugged. Men are strange. This man was stranger than most, but in a good way.

The beach house was a wooden affair, up on pilings to allow for the storm surges which accompany the Atlantic hurricanes. There were three levels and decks all around, lots of privacy.

The second level side deck included a hot tub, and Nancy couldn't wait to get in there and enjoy the view of the wide, bleak beach going for miles in each direction, the late afternoon sky as it faded to gray.

Nancy got out of her clothes and walked out onto the deck in just her wedgie sandals. Those long legs of hers looked amazing, and of course everything else about her looked amazing as well, perched up on top of those wedgies with the straps wrapped up around her ankles. The girl was completely at ease with nudity, totally confident. Leon got in the hot tub, kicked back and drank in the full glory of her naked body. He could tell that she obviously trusted him and was comfortable with his company.

'She's a stripper, of course,' Leon thought. If he had body as beautiful as hers, he'd walk around naked all day as well. "Okay," Leon said, "I guess we're at the boyfriend-girlfriend stage now."

Nancy joined him in the hot tub, sat on his lap and planted a big wet smacker on him. Leon's hands moved around her incredible curves, down around her wondrous hips to squeeze her tight, round ass. With his hands full of the most beautiful girl in the world, sitting butt naked on his lap, Leon was feeling like he'd just won the lottery.

A good-looking girlfriend will make a guy feel like that, and Leon hadn't had a girlfriend in quite a while. A long while, too long for him to want to think about. He still didn't know if he trusted Nancy, at least not completely. A thousand psychic wars had left his emotional blast shields almost permanently up, in the battle stations mode. Still, Nancy was making all the right noises, and her upbeat attitude was a big plus. Like she said herself, she might be a dancer, but she wasn't stupid.

They went inside to relax, and this of course involved a mild callisthenic, after which they both zonked out.

Leon came to about an hour later. Nancy was still out like a light, sleeping like a log. He got up, cleaned up a bit, went out to the kitchen. The turkey was in the sink, just unfrozen enough for him to slit open the plastic wrapping, reach in and remove the neck, liver and gizzard parts from the inside of the turkey. He then retrieved the device from the improvised Faraday bag, re-wrapped it in layers of aluminum foil, then double bagged it in sturdy zip lock bags, and jammed it inside the turkey. Then he re-sealed the turkey in plastic, secured with some extra heavy duty duct tape, and placed the entire affair into the freezer.

Then Leon sat down to see if he could do some thinking. He opened up his laptop but that turned out to be a distraction, so he pulled out a notebook and a pen and tried to make sense out of all the shit that had been going down over the past few days.

The pen and notebook wasn't doing it for him, either. Something was distracting him. Leon couldn't focus right now and then it occurred to him that he knew exactly what it was.

The girl.

Other than extremely brief encounters, Leon hadn't had a steady girlfriend or any kind of romance in years and he wasn't sure he wanted anything like this in his life right now. Strippers are notorious for messing with guys heads. Something about being up on stage and worshipped by crowds of guys, that and the lonely lifestyle they'd signed up for, made everything all about themselves. Leon didn't blame them, really. Strippers are total mercenaries, out to make as much as they can selling themselves, one way or another.

But this girl Nancy was coming across different, somehow. Maybe.

* * *

Lying together in the afterglow, Nancy rolled on her side and faced Leon. "What are we, Leon?"

"We're two lost souls, swimming in a fishbowl, year after year," Leon quoted.

"No, I mean, really," Nancy went on. "Are we lovers?"

"Of course we are lovers," Leon replied.

"I mean, are we in love?" she asked.

"I don't know."

"What do you mean you don't know? How can we be lovers if we are not in love?"

Drowning Creek

"Simple, I guess," Leon answered. "We make love, but to be in love must be more than just the physical act of love. I mean, we hopped into bed with one another the night we met, if you recall."

"Well, yes," Nancy replied. "That was sport sex. But isn't this more like the real thing?"

"I think it requires more than just an intimate knowledge of one another's bodies to know if you're in love with someone."

"What do you mean?"

"Well, is love unconditional? What if you became aware I'm guilty of some kind of heinous crime, or if I said or wrote some outrageous things?"

"Like what?"

"I dunno. What if you found out I'm a Nazi?"

"Are you a Nazi?"

"No, of course not. I'm just throwing that out there as an example."

"What about me," she asked, "doesn't it bother you that I'm dancing on stage and shakin' it for a bunch of sex-starved G.I.'s and dirty old men?"

"Not really," Leon said. "It's kind of a turn on, actually."

"How so?"

"When I see you up there peeling off your string-kini, stripping down and baring yourself in front of all those guys, and they're throwing money at you and going totally crazy over you, but I know you're coming home with me, well, that's a kind of a turn-on, actually."

"Hmmm. So we're lovers, but we don't know about love. Are we boyfriend-girlfriend?"

"Yes, I'm quite sure we've gotten there," Leon said. For some reason, what would normally be an uncomfortable or awkward conversation with a woman was not uncomfortable, nor awkward, with this girl. He honestly liked Nancy. "I don't know about love," he said, "but it's a strong like, that's for sure."

Nancy smiled and kissed him.

Dating a stripper is usually a psycho-dramatic nightmare, like walking through a minefield packed full of emotional Bouncing Betty anti-personnel landmines. But there was something about Nancy that was different, something that Leon liked about her. Something he liked about her so much that he didn't mind the pathway they were starting to walk together.

"You've got your walls up," Nancy said.

"That's exactly what I've got up," Leon answered.

"Why?"

Leon paused before he replied. "Nancy, there's a part of me you will never understand, no matter how well you get to know me. Nobody will understand that part of me except me, the guys I served with, and other veterans, no matter where they served or how long ago.

"I mean, its not as if I did anything particularly heroic," Leon continued. "I didn't storm Omaha Beach or anything like that – what I saw and did was miniscule by comparison. I don't have nightmares and wake up screaming, '*Blood! Blood!*' or anything like that, although I do know a guy who does. But I

Drowning Creek

broke a lot of trail, and only the guys who have walked those trails will know and understand. The long hours and days and weeks preparing for something, waiting for it to happen. Then doing it, enduring it, and then waiting and hoping to come home, and then dealing with it afterwards, the memories and the little things that remind you of it, that is something only the guys who have been through something like that will ever get."

"Nobody ever said it like that before," Nancy said. "Now I think I understand my father better."

"Maybe I can explain it better this way," Leon went on. "After I joined the Army and made it through Basic and Jump School, I went home on leave. Everyone treated me like a hero, even though I hadn't done anything yet. I even got together with my high school girlfriend, but things had cooled off and it was weird for both of us. After I'd been in the Army for about a year and a half, been assigned to a regular unit and been deployed, I went back home on leave. Everyone treated me like a hero all over again, but this time I had actually been somewhere and done something and I'm looking at the guys I'd gone to school with, played football with, and they were still hanging around town. A few were in college but most of the guys I ran with were doing things like driving a forklift or driving a delivery van and the big thing in their lives was working on their cars. They were shacking up with their high school girlfriends, getting married even.

"Meanwhile, I'd been out there on the other side of the planet, carving my name with my bayonet onto the walls of history. My high school buddies would look at me with smiling faces, bright shining eyes and I'd look at them and see nothing but emptiness in their eyes. They didn't know what I knew, hadn't seen the things I'd seen, and they never would."

Leon paused for a moment. "After a while, I stopped going home. The Army was my home now. The guys to the left and right of me, I had more in common with them than with my own family. There are guys who sign up, join the military right after high school because of the flag, and Mom and apple pie. I guess I was one of them. There's guys like that in every small town in America, and if you cut them, they bleed red, white and blue, and that's honorable. But after a while it's different. There's a breed of guys who, after they stay in long enough, when you cut one of them he bleeds green, camouflage-colored blood.

"That's me, that's what I morphed into. For guys like us, for the rest of our lives whenever we're away from the military we might as well be a lost soul in a sea of civilian strangers who will never understand, never in a million years, what kind of person we are."

"Woah," Nancy said quietly. "I think I get it. Now I know exactly what it was that I saw, with my Dad."

"Yeah," Leon said. "You said I've got walls up. Now you know what those walls are. You can throw yourself at those walls and you'll always bounce off. Maybe someday you can climb over the wall and meet me on the other side, but the wall will always be there, and you will never fully understand what it's made out of, and what guys like me went through, building that wall, brick by brick, stone by stone, ~~and~~ sandbag by sandbag."

Leon closed his eyes. His thoughts went involuntarily to the things he saw every day and every night in his head, things that he could not say anything about, things that could never be unseen. The sight of human bodies torn apart by explosives, by shrapnel. The decapitations.

Drowning Creek

Nancy leaned forward, closed her eyes, and kissed Leon on the lips. He returned her kiss. The time for talk was over.

XIII

Leon's phone rang. "Hello?"

"This is Major Caulfield. Group S-2."

"Yes sir," Leon answered. He wanted to say '*I'm standing at attention, sir,*' but he kept his mouth shut.

"It's time to go see C.I." Counter-Intelligence. "You know where they're at?"

"Not really, no."

"Its out on Armistead Street. 525th Military Intelligence Brigade headquarters. Over by the polo field."

"Do you have an address? I'll put it in my machine. I don't know that part of post, I never go there." Caulfield told him and Leon typed it into his map function.

On the way over he cruised past Gato's place, just to grab an eyeful, to see what he could see. There didn't appear to be anything out of the ordinary, other than a big white panel van in the driveway. Not new but not beat up. Leon didn't know if this was unusual or not, he'd never seen a van there before. He made a mental note. '*A big white van isn't your normal ride for tooling around town . . . a lot of crime can go down in a van.*'

Caulfield met Leon in the parking lot and they walked into the big headquarters building.

Drowning Creek

The C.I. guy's desk was as big as an aircraft carrier, with a big fancy nameplate – the kind guys would get done in the Philippines - carved out of wood in big, thick letters – 'Cecil Aldridge'. Leon imagined *'With a name like that, a guy's gotta become a spy guy.'*

Aldridge was an unassuming figure with neutral features. With his unremarkable appearance, from the nondescript haircut to the unassuming attire, it occurred to Leon that Aldridge could blend in seamlessly into any crowd - he was the quintessential 'Gray Man.'

Leon told Aldridge everything he'd told Johnson at CID, everything he'd told Caulfield. He started with pulling Ivy's lifeless body out of the creek, then he told them how he knew Ivy and everything he knew about Ivy. Then he told them about his first meeting with Lieutenant-Colonel Haglin, at the brig at Camp Lejeune, and the razor cuts all over Haglin's forearms, and what Haglin had told him about what had gone down, the confrontation when Ivy discovered that Haglin had been doing surveillance on her, her activities over at Gato's place.

"You think this Ivy woman was capable of doing something like this, cut a guy up with a straight razor?" Aldridge asked.

"I know she is," Leon replied, dead pan.

"What makes you say that?"

Leon told Aldridge about his encounter with ~~her~~ Ivy at the hospital, years ago, prior to finding Steve with his throat cut. Then he said what he and CID had found at Rudy's place – the pictures of Gato's place, the white vans.

Like before, the only thing he held back on was the device – the thing he'd found in the locker out at the airport. Until Leon understood what the hell it was, what it represented in the whole mix, something was telling him to keep the thing to himself.

Then Leon relayed what he'd seen at the No-Name gas station up on Deep River Road, what happened when he followed them down the road.

"You went up there?" Aldridge asked. "You did surveillance? That's a straight-up amateur move! You know how dangerous playing James Bond can be?"

"Yeah, I know," Leon replied. "That's why it was a one-off. There's no way I'm going back, setting up any kind of a pattern."

"Damn straight – not only is there the risk that if there is anything going on, if these guys actually are up to anything, they get spooked and go to ground, you could also end up very realistically dead."

"What, is anybody else keeping an eye on them?"

"I don't know. This is outside the mission of Army Counterintelligence."

"Is it? Let's see here – we've got a Colombian asshole who's a known ex-communist guerrilla, who has had extensive contact with members of US Army Special Forces, hanging out with a cabal of Middle Eastern weirdos of totally unknown status, and when an Army wife finds out that her husband is aware of their existence she goes ape shit, tries to kill her husband and ends up in Drowning Creek, graveyard dead. If that's not enough to pique your interest, what is?"

"Hmmm, okay. Kind of hard to argue, seeing as you put it that way."

"Okay, so now what?"

"Two things - we begin an investigation, and we reach out to other agencies – FBI, and because of the international aspect of this, they should inform CIA – to make sure we don't stumble into the middle of an ongoing investigation or surveillance operation. The most dangerous thing you can do in this business is end up having parallel operations, independent and ignorant of one another."

"Right."

"People can end up getting killed."

"Right," Leon said. "I want to be there when you talk to the Feds."

"Can't do that, you're not cleared to that level. Time to hand this over to the varsity team. The big boys."

"What the hell are you talking about," Leon said. "If it wasn't for me, you wouldn't even be aware of any of this. I'm cleared on the basis that I know what the hell is going on, I know all the players, I know where they live and I'm the one who alerted on what they might possibly be up to. It only makes perfect sense operationally to have the guy who's had eyes-on the target, to actually brief the fucking target."

"Hmmm. Okay." Aldridge looked at Caulfield, who looked absolutely noncommittal about the whole thing. They both knew that Leon was right, but Aldridge obviously didn't like it. Leon figured he was already up to his eyeballs in this thing and he was not going to let it go.

"So how we going to go about this?" Leon asked.

"First thing we do is we set up a meet and greet for you with the Bureau," Aldridge said. "Before we go over there, we're going to have to coordinate with your S-2," he looked at Caufield, who gave a perfunctory nod, "so they can send your clearance info over there, because the meeting will be in a SCIF."

"Right. Uh huh," Leon nodded.

"Also, before we go over there, you're going to give me a detailed brief on everything you've got, so all our ducks are in a row when we get there."

"Of course."

"Let's start by blocking the whole thing out on paper." Aldridge pulled out a yellow legal pad.

"Hang on," Leon said. "I've got an idea."

"What?"

"I can't think in this room, it's stifling my creativity. Why don't we go take a drive? A change of scenery might serve to jog the memory, boost the imagination, add a little juice to our planning process."

"Where do you want to go?"

"Deep River Road."

"Didn't I just finish telling you not to do any James Bondian stuff?" Aldridge was incredulous. "Besides, if you go back, you're establishing WAY too much of a pattern."

"It ain't James Bondian if YOU do it," Leon said. "They haven't seen you - you've never been to the No-Name gas

Drowning Creek

station. You can drop me off at a Waffle House or something, go scope out the place for yourself, then come back and tell me what you think."

"You really have a hard-on for these guys, don't you?"

"Listen, a friend of mine is looking at life in prison over something that's got something to do with whatever's going on with Gato and his crew of Iranian muldoons. I want to know whatever the hell it is they're up to, whatever the hell it is that drove Ivy to go berserk on Haglin and caused him to kill her in self-defense."

"You really think it's self-defense?" Aldridge asked.

"That's the only thing that makes sense, and the only thing that's keeping me from doing my own personal James Bond act on these guys is you and the resources you represent, to include Federal law enforcement and whoever you can scoop in from the intelligence community."

Alderidge looked at Leon for a minute while he considered all of this. "Okay," he finally said. "We'll go out there and I'll have a look around, see these guys for myself. Couldn't hurt anything." He looked at Caulfield. "You coming along?"

"No, I'm just passing this thing over to you," Caulfield said. "This is your football to run with. My work here is done."

"Okay," Aldridge replied. Then looking at Leon, "When do you want to go out there?"

"I'm free now," Leon shrugged.

* * *

They drove in silence for a while until they'd cleared base and were driving through the seemingly endless stands of pine trees, punctuated every quarter of a mile or so by a clearing with a trailer and a yard full of crap and beat up cars up on blocks out in front of it. Aldridge finally spoke up.

"Let's go over what do we know, and what do we not know."

"We know Gato is an ex-communist guerrilla from Colombia," Leon stated, "a sort of military grifter who's ingratiated himself and latched on to every mobile training team that's shown up down there over the past fifteen years, and now he's up here in the vicinity of Fort Bragg. That is weird just in and of itself."

"Granted."

"We know that he's hanging out with a posse of mysterious Iranians. Double extra weird."

"Right, but we know nothing about these guys. For all we know, they're exchange students."

"IRANIAN exchange students?" Leon exclaimed. "We have a student exchange program going with that place?"

"Okay, point taken."

"We know that Ivy was somehow involved with these guys."

"Right, but we don't know what."

"Right," Leon went on. "But what I do know is that Ivy was as crazy as a shithouse rat. Or at least, she had a real dark side and was capable of extreme violence . . ."

"Right."

"... and when she became aware that Haglin was aware of her hanging out with Gato and his crew, she went berserk, whipped out her straight razor and started slicing and dicing on her own husband."

"That is beyond extraordinary, right there," Aldridge admitted.

"That's what I'm saying. So what we've got is a bunch of question marks – things that just don't add up – and when you've got a bunch of pieces of a puzzle that don't fit, that don't make any sense, you've got to look for what's the sense that all of this makes."

"Right. On the other hand, it could be nothing."

"I doubt it," Leon said, "I really don't think so. Too much craziness, too much weirdness, and Ivy's actions really point a finger, some kind of indicator that something bigger is going on. It just doesn't make sense she'd go bonkers like that, just go totally apeshit and start slashing her own husband."

Aldridge was silent while he digested this. He finally spoke up, "When nothing makes sense, when you've got a bunch of puzzle pieces that don't fit, that don't make any sense, you've got to look for whatever it is that makes sense."

"Right."

"Okay, I'll drop you off at the Waffle House," he said.

"Okay," Leon agreed.

Peter Crittenden

* * *

Leon sat at the Waffle House, taking his time over a pecan waffle, bacon, and too many cups of coffee. Finally the waitress said, "Can you settle up? I'm ending my shift."

Leon said, "Sure," and he went up to the cash register, paid his bill and handed the waitress a fiver for a tip.

"I'm going to hang around for a while, I'm waiting for my ride to show up."

"That's fine. Do you want any more coffee?"

"No thanks. If I drink any more coffee my head will explode. Can I have a glass of water?"

"Sure."

He went back to looking at his phone and waiting for Aldridge to show up. He finally did show up, sat down across from Leon. A new waitress showed up. "Do you want a cup of coffee?"

"Sure, thanks."

"Do you want to look at a menu?" It was lunch time.

"Sure, I guess." Aldridge looked over at me. "You having anything?"

"I already ate while I was waiting for you."

Cecil looked at the menu and ordered a burger.

"What did you see up there?" Leon asked.

"No-Name gas station," he replied. "Filled up, went inside to pay. Three Middle Eastern dudes behind the counter.

Nothing out of the ordinary for any no name gas station brand X convenience store, I guess."

"Describe the guys behind the counter."

"Tall, taller than me. Dark hair, almost curly. All three of them needed a haircut, bad. Unshaven, one of them had a beard. Short beard, cropped close. The other guys looked like they shaved maybe once every two weeks."

"Okay, Gato wasn't there. What else did you see?"

"What is this," Aldridge asked, "an interrogation?"

"This is a debrief," Leon replied. "I'm trying to see what you saw, through your eyes, and possibly jog your memory as to something you might have seen but didn't stick out to you, so you didn't mention it. What did you see up there, out and around the gas station?"

"Hmmm, okay. There's a service building, two bays for working two vehicles, jam packed full of crap – old parts, wheels and tires, shit like that."

"Right. Anything else? What kind of cars or vehicles were parked around the place?"

"Three white vans."

"What kind of vans?"

"Panel vans. The bigger kind, not minivans. Those things they call club vans, at the rental agency."

"Three identical vans?"

"Yes, GMC's."

"Were they doing anything to the vans? Any activity around the vans?"

"Two other guys – they looked like brothers of the trio inside the convenience store - were working on them."

"What do you mean working on them? Working on all three vans, all at once?"

"Yes."

Leon got quiet.

"What?" Aldridge asked. "What's the big deal about white vans?"

"I don't know," Leon said, "it may or may not be anything."

"What are you thinking?"

"I'm thinking, three identical vehicles – white vans – that's got to be some kind of indicator right there, but indicator of what I have no idea," Leon said. "Three identical vehicles, that sound exactly like the white van I saw over at Gato's place when I drove past this morning. So that's four identical vehicles, and they're working on three of them. All at the same time. Does that sound a little out of the ordinary to you?"

"What do you mean?"

"Think about it," Leon said. "One white van parked on a driveway, there's nothing unusual about that. Three identical white vans all needing repairs or service at exactly the same time, at a no-name gas station out in the middle of nowhere? And the first white van, over where they live, that actually makes it four white vans. At least."

"What are you thinking?" Aldridge asked.

"I'm thinking this isn't just pulling maintenance on a van, it's more like prepping the vans, kitting them out before they go operational."

"You know," Aldridge said, looking at me over his coffee cup. "That actually might make sense."

"Thank you."

"Makes sense if you're paranoid or delusional or something, that is," Aldridge added sartorially.

"Thank you," Leon said, "and fuck you very much."

"That's okay," Aldridge replied. "These days, just looking at the headlines makes me wonder if I'm going crazy, and if I dare speak up about what's going on in the media, I have to keep throwing out a caveat: 'I'm not crazy, I don't think the world is flat, I'm not a conspiracy nut, NASA didn't stage the moon landings we really did go to the moon.' But there's so much crazy shit going on in the world right now that if you listen to yourself discussing it, you sound nuttier than Jim Carrey on LSD."

"Good to know I'm not the only one who's thinking that way," Leon said, sardonically.

"Yeah, I'd say you've pointed out enough random indicators, between Ivy going ape shit on her old man, to this Gato character and his crew of Iranian henchmen – or whatever the fuck they are – and now this fleet of strange white vans suddenly appearing, we've got something to give the Feds, something for them to look at. At least some kind of start point."

"Thank you," Leon said. It's good to know I'm not coming across as paranoid."

"Oh, you're coming across as paranoid all right. But don't worry about it. You know what they say," Aldredge smiled.

"Just because you're paranoid doesn't mean they aren't out to get you," Leon replied.

"Exactly."

XIV

Bright and early next morning Leon got a call from Cecil. "Hey. This is Aldridge."

"To what do I own this great honor?"

"Ha. Check it out – I'm calling to let you know the FBI will be dropping by your place."

"Thanks for the heads up. Should I grab my shotgun, or my rifle?"

"That's why I'm calling – it's a courtesy visit, they're coming around because I asked them, to help expedite getting your clearance into their system. Don't go full snake eater on them."

"That's unusual – the big boys coming to me," Leon said. "They usually expect us to go crawling to them."

"Take it as a professional compliment. I went to them, showed them everything you and Caulfield showed me – all the pics, your notes – told them about what I saw at the No-Name gas station."

"Okay, thanks for the heads up. Tell you what, I'll get dressed. I might actually shave."

"They're interested in what you have to say," Aldridge said. "They're interested in the situation, and they're actually interested in your involvement, if this thing turns into an investigation."

"Don't worry, I'll be professional. I won't fuck with them," Leon said.

"Attaboy."

"... too much, that is."

"Ha!" Aldridge snorted.

"It's all good," Leon said. "One fight, one team, right?"

"Exactly!"

Five years ago, Leon would have been totally cool about working with the Feds, totally cooperative. But that was before everything started going off the rails, at the highest levels. *'It's a whole new world out there now,'* Leon thought *'and not necessarily a better one.'* 'One fight, one team' was General Flynn's attitude when he had his little chat with the Bureau, and look where it got him. Leon would be courteous with the Feds, professional, but they were going to have to earn his trust.

Right on cue the doorbell rang. *'This is going to be interesting,'* Leon thought.

Leon answered the door. The two men standing there whipped out badges and introduced themselves - Special Agents McBride and Special Agent Kleckner. They were wearing polo shirts, light windbreakers, tan tactical pants with cargo pockets and random straps and buckles, Oakley sunglasses and 1950s law enforcement haircuts - the corporate 'business casual' look. To Leon, the guys looked like Special Agents Smith and Jones.

"You guys are dressed way too smooth for this neighborhood," Leon told them. "This is Fayette-Nam. You need to show up in your roughs when you come this deep into enemy territory."

Kleckner and McBride just looked at him, stone faced.

"Agent Aldridge told us what you've got. What can you tell us, in your own words?"

For a split second Leon felt like saying, *'Not without a warrant, and not without a lawyer'*, but then he thought *'Fuck it, I don't want to be counterproductive, I'm the one who actually wants to sic these guys onto Gato.'* He figured if the conversation turned into an interrogation he could tell them to go fuck themselves, but until then he was willing to try and make some traction on this thing.

"Come inside, I'll get you some coffee."

Sitting around the kitchen nook table over cups of coffee, Kleckner said, "Agent Aldridge contacted your security office yesterday afternoon, got us verification of your clearance."

"That was fast," Leon said. "He must be eager to get rid of me, hand me off to you guys."

So Leon told them everything, from the beginning. He showed them the pics he'd brought over from Haglin's place, how he knew Haglin, how he knew Ivy. He told them about Gato, how he knew Gato, and Gato's fucked up background. He told them how Ivy had gone bonkers when Haglin confronted her about Gato and his crew of Iranians, the white vans, everything. The only thing Leon didn't throw in there was the device, of course, and the situation that happened the other day, the gun battle in front of his house. He didn't think it was part of anything connected.

"You don't think you're crazy or paranoid?"

"Aldridge and I actually discussed that, just yesterday," Leon grinned. "The way things are going out there in the world these days, anything and everything any of us say, speak or do makes us look fucking crazy. But the answer is no, I don't think I'm crazy. I think this falls well within the 'If You See Something, Say Something' department."

"Hmmm, okay. I guess we'll look into it."

"Good," Leon said. "What's the next step?"

"Not you," McBride said. "Your job is done, we'll handle it from here."

"Fuck that. I'm already into this thing up to my eyebrows."

"What do you mean?"

"A girl I know is dead. Her husband – my friend – is facing charges for her murder, and this all came out of her going into psycho-killer mode over seeing pictures of herself going in and out of Gato's house. I'm the one who figured these guys are up to something – God knows what – and I'm not backing down or letting off until I know what the fuck is going on."

"If you jeopardize this investigation, it will mean Federal charges," Kleckner said, frowning.

"I'm not going to jeopardize shit – I'm a professional, too. The last thing I'm going to do is snoop around on those guys, I've done that and I'm not going to get painted by them, alert them to any hint they're being watched. But you guys need me."

"Why do we need you, Sergeant Leonard?"

"First of all, you guys can call me Leon, or you can give me a fucked up nickname, or a code name, or whatever you want. Nobody calls me 'Sergeant Leonard' unless I'm getting my ass chewed. I'm not going to call you guys Special Agent what's-yer-face every time we have to say pass the salt or whatever.

"What you need is my perspective," Leon continued. "You need to pick my brain. You need to run shit past me. I'm a soldier, you're policemen - we look at things differently. An extra set of eyes and ears, another brain in the mix, is not a bad thing. Besides, I'm the guy who can make Gato and his crew, for you. You've never laid eyes on these guys, all you know is what you've seen from just looking at these black and whites," Leon said, indicating the pics in the file they'd laid on the table desk. "I can at least confirm for you who you're looking at when you're looking at him."

"Hmmm." McBride and Kleckner looked at each other.

"And how many Farsi speakers you got around here? I can actually understand what these motherfuckers are saying. Is Washington going to send in a speaker on the basis of what you've got so far?"

"You have a point there."

"Yeah," Leon said. He didn't add that he represented another gun in the mix, thirty percent more firepower if this thing was ever to go dynamic. "And you've got my clearance," he added, "so you know I'm cleared to Ridiculous Level, at echelons above Reality."

"If you're going to work with us, you're going to have to get serious," McBride said sternly.

"You guys need to lighten up," I said. "If you're wound this tight sitting around the table having coffee, how are you going to be when the bullets start flying on the two-way shooting range?"

"Okay, you're on the case," Kleckner said. "Got anything else to add?"

Now Leon told them about the exchange of gunfire, with the guy who drove up on his lawn.

"Jeez," Kleckner said. "Why didn't you tell us about that before."

"I really didn't think it was relevant. I didn't want to muddy the waters about what we know and what we think we're looking at with Gato and his band of merry men. Then I thought I might as well tell you, in case it comes up while you're doing your due diligence on me."

"Not relevant!" McBride exclaimed. "How on Earth can a shootout in front of your house not be relevant?"

"Well, you know we call this place FayetteNam. Now you know why."

"Okay," Kleckner said. "Anything else?"

"There actually is one more thing," Leon said.

"Whaddya got?"

"We've got this thing called Eagle Eye." Eagle Eye is a planning tool, developed by the Air Force, which provides satellite overhead of anywhere and everywhere.

"We've got Eagle Eye as well," McBride replied.

"Really? That's cool. Then we need to go to your office, look at the No-Name gas station on Eagle Eye, and see what we can see," Leon said. "In the meantime, I've got a favor to ask of you guys."

"What's that?"

"It's one fight, one team, right?"

"Yes, of course."

"Let's get on these guys," Leon said. "Watch them like a hawk on a field mouse. There's more to know about what's going on, I've barely scratched the surface. We need to keep an eye on these guys because whatever they're up to, sooner or later they're going to go dynamic and we don't know when, but I have my suspicions."

"Well you know we have other cases we're working and we haven't officially opened an investigation on this, yet," McBride said.

"Well then, open one," Leon shot back. "This shit smells fishy as the docks at low tide and the clock is ticking, we don't have time for bureaucratic bullshit."

Leon caught a split-second blink in Kleckner's eye – the pun was not lost on him.

"Gato and his crew are up to something," Leon went on, "Something beyond evil and they're doing it practically right out there in the open, for God and everyone to see. We need to keep our fingers on the pulse of this thing. Think about it. It sure would look pretty bad if, after all hell breaks loose and we've got bodies all over the place, for me to be interviewed on national TV saying, 'I knew this was going to happen, this is what I had on the guys, and when I alerted the FBI to it, they blew me off.'"

"You've got a point," Kleckner said.

Leon couldn't believe how smooth this interview was going. A little voice in the back of his head was saying he was being walked down the primrose path, but it wasn't setting off alarm bells or anything. They were still in the dog-sniffing stage, but so far everything about these guys smelled okay. "We really don't want to fuck this thing up," he said.

"We actually looked at Eagle Eye yesterday, after Aldridge spoke to us," McBride said. "Scoped out the No-Name gas station."

"Yeah, what did you see?"

"Didn't see anything illegal."

Leon shrugged. "It ain't illegal to hang out around a gas station," he said. "That doesn't mean a person isn't up to no good. Did you see any white vans?"

"Yeah. Four white vans."

"Anything unusual about them?" Leon asked. "Other than the fact there are four, non-descript white panel vans parked at a no-name gas station, and maybe a fifth one parked on the driveway at Gato's house?"

"They appear to be doing something with them. Something weird, not normal."

"Yeah, what?"

"We can't really talk here," McBride said. "We need to continue this conversation in a SCIF."

Right at that moment, Nancy came walking out of the bedroom towards the kitchen. Nancy was only wearing black lace bra and panties – which for her was practically overdressed – a skimpy G-string thong panty, actually, and a barely-there bra that left almost nothing to the imagination. Kleckner and McBride's heads snapped around and their eyes practically bulged out of their sockets. Leon thought they were going to dislocate their necks.

"Oh hey, Hon," Leon said when Nancy returned from the kitchen with a cup of coffee. "These are some guys I'm working with. I'm going over their office soon. Can you lock the place up and set the alarm before you go?"

Nancy leaned back against the counter that separated the kitchen from the dining room. She was smiling over her cup of coffee, practically posing. "Sure, Hon," she said. Nancy knew exactly the effect her body was having on the guys. Hypnotizing men with her curves was her superpower, and she was loving every second of it.

"We might as well get down to your office and look at Eagle Eye," Leon said. "I want to see what it is you guys saw."

No response from Agents Smith & Jones.

"Guys. GUYS!"

XV

After Kleckner and McBride left, Nancy came up to Leon. "What's going on?"

"What do you mean?" Leon asked.

"Your walls are up again," Nancy said.

"Yeah," Leon shrugged.

"Tell me what's going on," she said. "First that crazy guy comes around and shoots at you, then these two guys who totally look like cops."

"They're Feds," Leon said. "FBI."

"Tell me what's going on."

"Well, I can't tell you everything, in fact I'm not sure I can tell you anything, because I don't understand what's going on myself. Not yet, at least."

"What do you mean by that? Are you in some kind of trouble, Leon?"

"I don't think so. I really don't know," Leon said. "A lot of crazy stuff has been happening, one crazy thing after another, and I'm having a hard time believing myself; what everything is pointing to, where it's all going."

"Hmmm," said Nancy. "Maybe I can help."

"Go on."

"Well, maybe the way to think it out is to put all the cards on the table, all the parts and pieces and talk it out."

"Could be," Leon admitted. "But it's so damn complex that I don't even know where to start."

"You know how, when a problem or a set of circumstances are so complex and confusing – one thing piled up upon another – a good method to sort things out is to stand back, way back, and look at everything with some kind of perspective?"

"Yes," Leon said. "We call that the one-over-a-million eye view, or the C-and-C bird point-of-view," Leon said.

"C-and-C bird?"

"Command and Control. The commander hovers over the battlefield in a helicopter and manages the thing like a conductor, leading an orchestra."

"Um, okay," Nancy said.

* * *

Leon turned on the TV, one of the cable news channels. It was a weather segment at the end of the hour. The graphic showed the symbol for a hurricane, and it was heading right for the coast, the same place Leon and Nancy had just spent the last few days. "The hurricane is slowing down, gathering strength before it makes landfall," the announcer was saying. "We're expecting a Cat 3 at least but it will probably pick up to a Cat 4, which means widespread flooding all along the Outer Banks, significant property damage and probably loss of power over an extensive area."

"Oh shit," Leon said quietly.

"What?" Nancy looked at him.

"Loss of power."

"Yes, it will be terrible," Nancy said. "Won't they be evacuating the Outer Banks?"

"Yes, which actually makes it worse."

"What do you mean?"

"I gotta go out there."

"What are you talking about?"

"I left something out there and I've got to go back, pick it up."

"What on Earth are you talking about?" Nancy asked.

"The turkey," Leon replied.

"The TURKEY?"

"Yeah. I left it in the freezer," Leon stated. "There's going to be power outages and the caretaker is going to come and throw out all the food in the freezer, so I've got to go and fetch the turkey before it gets tossed out with everything else."

"Leon, there's a Cat 3, possibly a Cat 4 hurricane bearing down on that place!" Nancy said. "The whole place is going to be underwater with the storm surge, all hell will be breaking loose, and you're worried about a frozen turkey?"

"It's not the turkey, it's what I put in it. I used the turkey as a stash, and now I've got to go get it back before the power goes out and they throw out everything in the freezer."

"Oh shit," said Nancy. "What are we talking about here? Drugs?"

"No, of course not."

"Money?"

"No. I'm not exactly sure what it is, but it's pretty important and seems valuable enough that people want to kill for it."

"What on Earth are you talking about, Leon?" Nancy said, again.

"I'm not sure, but I've got to get out to the Outer Banks before they close all the bridges out there, and get that damn bird."

"Oh shit," Nancy moaned. "All you special ops guys are crazy. You're just like my Dad. He does crazy shit like this all the time. What is it with you guys?"

"I gotta go out there, Nancy," Leon said grimly. "I gotta do this thing."

"Oh hell," Nancy moaned.

* * *

Leon went outside and threw a bag in the back of his truck. The air was heavy, almost wet - Leon could feel the barometric pressure dropping in his bones. A tearful Nancy bade him farewell, "Please be careful, Honey," she said. In his head, Leon could hear what she'd left unsaid – *'You're all I've got.'*

Sometimes it seemed to Leon he was saying goodbye to people, all his life.

Leon knew instinctively this storm was winding up to be more powerful than the news predicted. He knew under normal circumstances what he was planning to do would be pure insanity, but this was not the time to play it safe. It was time to get focused and drive on.

XVI

Leon headed to the coast. Along the way there the storm intensified. Intermittent bouts of heavy rain lashed at the windshield of his truck as the outer edges of the storm made landfall. It was noon but the sky was gray, dark and foreboding. The pine trees were blowing around, branches and other debris were starting to blow onto the roadway.

Leon wasn't kidding himself – they'd have the causeways to the Outer Banks closed off, in fact they were in the process of evacuating the beach towns - but he figured if there was any way to get out there, he would figure it out. Whatever that thing was, it was valuable enough for Ivy to want to kill Rudy over it, and he was beginning to suspect that asshole who'd fired at him the other day had something to do with it as well. The thing had some kind of value, it was the clue as to why Ivy had tried killing Rudy and was possibly the thing that would get Rudy off the hook for killing her, in self-defense. Leon could not risk losing it.

Sure enough, up ahead loomed a roadblock. Several State Trooper cars with their lights flashing. Leon pulled to a stop. When the Trooper came up, Leon lowered his window. A gust of wind blew rain into his truck.

"Turn around, go back," the Trooper said. "Nobody's going out to the beach. The whole place is under evacuation orders, from the Governor."

Drowning Creek

"Yes, sir," Leon said. He backed up, did a U-turn and headed back to the last gas station. The gas station was by the water, along one of the inlets. There was a small marina there, maybe he could get a boat.

Leon parked and went into the shop. The guy behind the counter said, "You're lucky, you got here just in time. We're about to shut down." He indicated with a nod of his head to the weather outside, "For the storm."

"Thanks," said Leon. "I need a boat, by the way."

"A what?"

"A boat. Can you rent me a boat?"

"Are you fucking crazy, Mister? There's a hurricane going on out there!"

"It's not here yet, and yes, in fact, I am kind of crazy. Can you rent me a boat?"

"Mister, I'd be crazy to rent you a boat!"

Leon reached into his pocket, pulled out his billfold, and started peeling off hundred-dollar bills, laying them down on the counter in front of the man. By the time he laid the sixth hundred down on the counter, the man said, "Listen, Mister. I don't know who you are or what's your game, but I can't rent you a boat right now, not with this storm bearing down. But I tell you what – if you absolutely, positively must have a boat, maybe I'll sell you one."

"Good enough," Leon said. "What do you got, and how much is it?"

The man came around the counter and they both walked out to the back of the store, where the marina was. He pointed at a twenty-four-footer, with a center console and two Mercury 120 outboards. "It's going to cost you a little more than six hundred, Mister. That won't even make the down payment."

"I don't have enough cash on me. How about we do a swap? My truck for your boat?"

The man looked over at Leon's truck. "She's a 2019 Dodge Ram 2500, Cummins diesel engine, all tricked out, in good shape," Leon said.

The man thought about it for a second. "Okay, that sounds fair."

"Can I come back later and get my stuff out of the truck? I gotta get out to the Outer Bank, now," Leon said.

"Sure, Mister."

"Tell you what, sir," Leon said. "I really don't want to buy a boat right now. Can I just borrow your boat and leave my truck as collateral? I'll pay you a thousand dollars, and if I don't come back, the truck is yours. If I do come back, you get your boat back, I get my truck back and either way you pocket a thousand dollars."

The man thought about it for a moment.

"Look, it's a win-win," Leon said. "If I don't get back, you get a truck and insurance pays for the loss of the boat."

"That sounds even better. You need anything else?"

"Well, I'm gonna need enough gas to get me out to the island and back, some food and water, and at least a twelve pack of beer."

Drowning Creek

"I'm gonna have to charge you for the gas and the supplies. That's not coming out of the thousand."

"Of course, not a problem."

"You're really crazy, Mister. You know that, right?"

"You have no idea, sir," Leon said, looking the man dead in the eye.

* * *

Leon grabbed his stuff out of the truck, grabbed some supplies out of the shop, topped off the fuel in the boat's inboard tanks, loaded two extra tanks into the boat and the swap was complete. The last thing they did was exchange phone numbers.

"At least tell me where you're going, mister," the man said, "so we'll know where to look for the boat." What was left unsaid - but Leon heard – was: *'So we'll know where to look for the body.'*

"Duck."

"Then just parallel the bridge over there," the man pointed to the causeway, barely visible through the curtains of rain, "and when you come to the other side of the sound, turn left and parallel the shore north a little bit and there's an inlet. On the other side you'll see the golf course. The golf course has a little marina, in an inlet. Moor the boat over there, it'll be protected from the storm."

"Good. Thanks," Leon hollered over the sound of the storm.

"And good luck, Mister. I hope I see you again," the man hollered back.

"Thanks," said Leon.

As he fired up the engines and pulled away from the dock, what was going through Leon's mind was points of failure - the obvious things like engine quitting, getting swamped by seas, running aground on a sand bar or running out of fuel or worst of all getting thrown from the boat with no dead man switch connected. He thought about how to find a boat mooring and hopefully getting back under way with the same working boat.

Leon thought of all the crazy things he'd done over the course of twenty years in Special Forces. A principle he'd followed was *'We do not gamble with our lives, but we take calculated risks.'* Dying is always a possibility but it has to be worth it. This wasn't even a calculated risk. This was just crazy.

The waters inside the marina were protected by the breakwater but there was still some chop - large craft bobbed up and down at their moorings like bathtub toys. As soon as he pulled into the open waters of the sound there were heavy swells. Leon popped open a can of beer. *'Might as well do this thing right,'* he thought.

Leon headed south a bit so he could keep visibility on the causeway. It was only two in the afternoon but the heavy rain and gray clouds made a darkness beyond the gray, a darkness so dark it almost looked like the sun had already gone down. The only thing that stood out was the white of the cresting waves. It was three miles across the sound according to his GPS, going thirty knots Leon figured he could make it in less than twenty minutes, but with the wind and rain and managing the craft through and over the heavy swells, he was chugging along at less than ten knots. *'This is gonna suck,'* he thought. *'Gonna take all frikkin' day to get there.'*

The wind and the rain were bad enough, but after he rounded the breakwater, cleared the channel and was out in the Albemarle Sound itself, the winds lashed at his face and the swells lifted the boat, tossing it around like a bathtub toy. Leon rode the back of a wave near the crest going in to prevent his craft from pitch poling, taking care as he turned the helm to avoid capsizing. A wave coming up from behind could drive the bow down into the trough of the wave, flipping the boat and crushing everything.

Leon momentarily questioned his own sanity. *'Maybe I shoulda waited 'til the storm lifted,'* he thought. *'Maybe it's not too late to turn back.'* Then, *'Fuck that, I'm committed. This ain't nuthin' but a really bad rainstorm. It's not as if I'm out on the open sea.'* Leon had ridden out a typhoon on an aircraft carrier once, off the coast of the Philippines. THAT had sucked, royal – even in a carrier. This was bad, but it was no way that bad; the Sound was relatively protected waters.

Now it was raining so hard the sky was full of water moving sideways at Leon. He couldn't see the far bank of the Sound, could barely see the causeway to the south of him, which he followed to make it to the other side. He was totally saturated, and the boat was filling up with water. He opened the stern self-bailers and drove on against the rain that blasted against him.

'There's only one way through this thing, only one way out of this thing,' Leon told himself. *'I've got to drive on. The only way out of this thing is to fight my way through it.'* Still, it was daunting. At times he could not even see the causeway to his right and trusted to the compass on the console. Glancing over his shoulder, Leon could no longer see the shore he'd left. All was gray, lost in curtains of rain driven by the powerful wind.

Peter Crittenden

The other shore finally loomed up ahead. Through the gray, driving rain it looked like it was almost half a mile away, but Leon judged the distance to be no more than a couple of football fields. Leon turned the boat north to parallel the shore, looking for the inlet. The heavier power of the storm coming off the outer bank reduced the visibility to almost zero. Leon slowed down and pulled closer to the shore. It was going to be difficult to spot the inlet with the wind and rain, he didn't want to miss it. Something made a noise, Leon turned to look and saw the inlet to his right, he had just passed it. Leon swung his craft around, nearly capsizing as a swell caught his beam.

The swells abated as Leon entered the channel. The mile-wide outer bank island provided a low windbreak, some relief from the power of the storm. There appeared to be a break in the storm and remarkably, visibility seemed to improve. As bad as crossing the Sound had been, it was nothing compared to the energy of the storm on the other side of the island. *'The seas must be boiling,'* Leon thought, looking east to the ocean side. All he could see was a turbulent gray mass of cloud and water swirling around where the horizon should be. The Atlantic off the Carolina coast is a super scary place in a storm. It's not called the Graveyard of the Atlantic for nothing - the seabed is littered with shipwrecks.

Leon proceeded up the channel. Up ahead he saw the small marina by the golf course, craft like his bobbing up and down in a sheltered cove. 'Thank God,' he thought. The first half of his ordeal was over. Or at least, the first third. He still had to get to the beach house, on foot, and then ride out the storm.

Leon pulled the boat into a vacant slip, grabbed a line and hopped over onto the dock, already pitching in the crazy water. He doubled up his lines and gave the moorings some

Drowning Creek

extra slack. Leon looked across the golf course. Sheets of rain made it impossible to see across to the beach road. He glanced back at the boat, hoped she'd still be there when he got back, but he doubted somehow that she would.

Leon set out across the golf course, leaning into the blowing storm.

The wind blew rain like liquid knife blades, Leon had to squeeze his eyes down to a narrow squint as he leaned into the storm. Heavy curtains of rain lashed at Leon, at times he could barely see across the golf course. '*Dammit,*' he thought as he staggered against the storm, '*I should've brought a goddamn compass.*' He figured he must be halfway across the golf course when a random thought crossed his mind; '*Here I am, the big bad Green Beret, barrel-chested freedom fighter, liberator of the oppressed, served on five continents, shot at on three, gonna die like a drowned rat in the middle of a golf course, on dry land.*' Then he thought, '*Well, nearly dry . . .*'

Leon finally made it to the far edge of the golf course. There were some trees and low shrubs, through which he could glimpse the street. Leon busted through the underbrush. Between the road and him was a drainage ditch which now was a raging torrent. A dead possum floated by. Leon looked left and right. There was an access road with a culvert. The water was up to the level of the road, but the road was passable. Leon made his way towards it.

From where he stood at the eastern edge of the golf course, Leon could see across the low outer bank to what was normally the beach. There was no horizon line between the sea and the sky, just a furious mass of gray cloud and water blowing all around. Leon was drenched but there was no going back, the only way out of this mess was to keep putting one foot in front of the other to make it to the beach house.

The streets were empty and the buildings dark, the result of the evacuation. It was about three p.m. - mid-afternoon – but the streetlights were on. Leon glanced down. The water was beginning to rise over the road he walked along, it was almost to his ankles. A long black snake swam by, a water moccasin. Bad actor, deadly poison. *'I won't bother you if you don't bother me,'* Leon thought as he leaned forward into the storm. The only way out of this thing was to make it to the beach house.

The water was over his ankles and rising; this was the storm surge, the wind blowing water ashore combined with the rising tide. *'Hurricane had to come same time as the full moon,'* Leon thought. Situation was going from bad to worse, Leon had to get to that beach house before the storm surge became a rising flood. A large mass of rats swam by – a veritable sea of little creatures that moved almost as a single lifeform, atop the floodwaters. Leon backed off, let the rodents go by before he continued. It was getting so that he could only see he was walking on the street by the presence of street signs, lamp posts and fire hydrants; the water was now up to mid-calf level. Leon staggered on.

Leon reached the road that paralleled the ocean side of the outer bank. There was no horizon, the sky and the sea were a furious mass of gray and black, Leon could barely make out the outlines of the structures lining the beach road. Going by where he'd landed and walked across the golf course, Leon turned left and walked north to find the beach house.

The storm was reaching its peak; Leon staggered through floodwaters up to mid-thigh level. Where before he encountered small animals, now cars were floating by. It occurred to Leon that if he'd waited a bit, he could have simply navigated the boat over the outer bank. For a brief moment, he considered actually going back to the boat, but then he figured he'd come too far and was nearly there. One thing for sure, Leon had to get to that beach house soon, things were getting totally out of control.

Finally he got there. *'Thank God,'* Leon thought. The flood waters were splashing halfway up the first flight of steps, up to the first level of the beach house, up on stilts. He grabbed the handrail just in time as a powerful gust nearly blew him off the stairs. After the first flight, the building itself sheltered him from the storm and he made it to the door. Leon easily picked the lock, and he was in.

XVII

Leon flipped on the lights – the power was still on, apparently, although he didn't expect that to last much longer. He went to the bathroom and grabbed a towel to dry off. The image looking back at him in the mirror looked like a bedraggled, crazy man. The phrase *'A drowned rat,'* crossed Leon's mind. *'Oh well,'* he thought, *'At least now I'll be a dry drowned rat.'*

Leon went to the freezer and took out the turkey. Mission accomplished. Or at least, the first half of the mission. The turkey was frozen solid, of course, and Leon couldn't get his hand into it to extract the device. Leon put the turkey in the sink and filled it with water to thaw the bird out a bit.

This was going to take hours. Leon figured what the hell, he wasn't going to eat the damn bird, he just needed to get the device out from inside of it. He put the kettle on the stovetop and started boiling water. Meanwhile he drained the cold water from the sink and opened up the hot water. Within minutes he was able to get his hand inside the bird and he retrieved the device. He threw away the outer zip lock bag and put the thing in his pocket.

Now he had to survive the storm. Leon went to a bedroom on the side of the beach house away from the blast of the storm, lay down and pulled the blanket over him. Right on cue, the power went out.

The storm howled through the night and the beach house swayed on its stilts, but it maintained. Sleep was nearly impossible with the big wind and rain, but Leon eventually passed out from sheer exhaustion. When he woke up it was deathly quiet. Leon got up and felt his way to a window. Outside it was dark, as black as hell, and the stillness was almost unnerving.

Leon knew the storm was not finished, the thing was only halfway through. This was the eye of the storm, the strongest part would be the eye wall, when it came. There were several hours of blast yet to endure. Leon went to the kitchen - he'd seen a bottle of whiskey there, last time, maybe it was still there. Thankfully, the bottle was there. Now was a good time for a shot.

The wall of the storm came over the beach and the house shook and groaned. Leon found his way into the hall bathroom, the smallest room in the house. He sat on the floor with his back against the wall, took another swig from the bottle and prepared himself for God only knew how many more hours of riding out the storm.

He could feel waves pounding against the wooden pilings of the beach house. Where once there had been land, the storm surge had become an angry sea. The house was really shaking and Leon wondered if it would hold up against the storm. 'This is beautiful,' Leon thought, sarcastically. '*A life of heroic action and adventure on six continents – shot at on three – and now I'm going to die trapped like an animal in a wooden shack on the beach in the middle of a Carolina hurricane.*' As the storm raged on, at some point, Leon somehow finally passed into merciful, black sleep.

Peter Crittenden

* * *

Sometime between midnight and dawn Leon awoke to the sound of the beach house creaking and groaning. The whole place ~~felt like it~~ was swaying. Leon put his hand down to the floor but it wasn't him, he hadn't drunk anywhere near enough whiskey to have the spins – the building itself was starting to rock, picking up momentum with every large wave that crashed into it, two stories below.

Leon was wide awake now. He made his way carefully to the front door, carefully opened it and shone his light down, beyond the landing and the stairs. The whole parking area beneath the building was a boiling mass of black water, with heavy waves surging against the uprights. The storm had several more hours until it passed, and Leon had nowhere to go. Leon closed the door, leaned against it, head down, and prayed.

The whole place kept rocking, and it only seemed to increase with the pounding of the waves below. Leon figured it was only a matter of time. Looking about the dark interior, Leon looked around. *'What is the sturdiest part of a house?'* Leon made his way to the small walk-in closet in the master bedroom, next to the bathroom. Feeling the building shake, Leon pulled the mattress off the queen-sized bed and stuffed it in the closet, up against one side. All the clothes hangers looked like a bad thing to get mixed up with, so he took them all down and tossed them to the furthest part of the room. Leon figured another mattress might be a good idea, to wrap up in like a cocoon. So he staggered down the hallway back to the small room he was in before, and dragged that mattress back to the walk-in closet. *'It doesn't get any better than this,'* he thought as he sandwiched himself in between the mattresses.

The whole house was beginning to creak and groan louder, and the movement of the structure was getting worse, more severe. Sleep was impossible. Leon was experiencing a kind of fear unlike anything he'd ever felt before. There was the kind of fear one feels before jumping out of an airplane in the middle of the night, the fear one feels before facing the enemy in combat, but there's always a point where the fight or flight dilemma gets overwhelmed because there's no way out of it and so the fear gets shelved and you just get on with what you're doing, and even though you know there's a chance you might get it, there's always some kind of control mechanism. This was different – there was no way he could fight the storm or even manage his odds of survival. If this house went over he was going with it and for now all he could do was hang on and pray for survival. The house was shaking now like crazy. Leon prayed to God he'd make it to see the sun come up.

Some kind of huge wave hit the side of the building like a slap, the wooden structure shook and then there was a loud SNAP – as loud as a rifle shot. Leon's eyes went wide. The building shook again and more loud snapping and crunching sounds followed. Leon hoped against hope that the movement he felt was his imagination but no – with a sinking feeling in his gut he realized the whole place was starting to lean over. '*Maybe it will stop*,' he thought with despair, knowing that it would not. A chain of events that was inevitable was starting to play out, and Leon knew he had no more control over this thing than if he was a rat on a sinking ship. The house was going over, and he was going with it.

Then there was another snap – this one like a small explosion - then a lot of crunching noises all at once and then things started moving so fast Leon couldn't even process time. The building lurched hard, then started going over. Leon clung to his mattresses and hoped he wouldn't get crushed, or worse, be submerged, stuck underwater somehow, to drown. Then with an almighty sound like a giant was sighing, the entire edifice piled over almost ninety degrees and there was crashing and smashing and splashing as the side of the building settled into the flood and the muck below. The cacophony was accompanied by the sounds of furniture crashing, the contents of cupboards crashing – plates and cups and glasses and silverware and pots and pans – and the thud of heavier objects like the refrigerator, washer and dryer crashing about. Then more snapping and popping as studs that were never intended to act as support beams snapped in half like toothpicks. And then the water came pouring in and splashing about.

In the darkness of the closet within his cocoon of mattresses, Leon felt his face, then ran his hands down his body. He was intact, nothing was broken. His nose was still where it belonged on his face, his arms and legs appeared uninjured, and - thankfully - his cock and balls were still there. He did not appear to be bleeding, he was not trapped and he was not impaled. As he crawled forward, attempting to extract himself from the closet, the first place he put his hand down landed in several inches of water. Oh shit. He had to get out of here, find a higher place.

Now not only was it dark but everything was sideways. What before were the walls were now the ceiling and the floor, and the doors and windows were on the floor. Leon collected his thoughts. Where once he had been on the third floor, now he was on the ground floor – the streets were flooding and inside this box he was trapped in the water was rising, it was up to his thighs and rising. He had to find a way up and out of this place. It was pitch black, he could only see where his headlamp shone, furniture was stacked haphazardly about making it all the more difficult and confusing – he was essentially stuck in a giant game of pick-up-sticks, inside a pitch-black box, and the water was rising fast.

Leon looked up. In the shine of his headlamp he saw - on what was now the ceiling - a door. That was his way up and out. Time to start stacking furniture. Trouble was, what was once one of the walls in a twenty-by-fifteen-foot room was now a twenty-foot ceiling, and there was only so much furniture. Leon sat on his stack of chairs and coffee tables and looked down at the reflection of his headlamp on the rising waters. '*Shit*,' he thought. '*All I gotta do is just sit here and sooner or later I'll be able to swim up to the door.*'

No longer up on stilts, now the house shook more than before as the big rollers coming over what used to be the beach slapped into what used to be the floor – which of course was now side of the house. This absolutely sucked, Leon's misery was immeasurable. Would the water break apart the building, and would he be trapped and crushed beneath falling studs or beams? The only consolation was the water seemed to have stopped rising. As he looked around the water still slopped about with the wave energy outside the house, and it appeared he was on an island of sticks of furniture in a crazy indoor sea.

An effect of the continual strain of adrenaline is overwhelming fatigue. Leon found himself nodding out, chin falling to chest, only to jerk his head up again, wide awake and yet beset by an uncontrollable yawning. The night wore on, the pounding of water against the walls and the rocking went on and on and on, it seemed like it would never stop.

It was a military situation . . . but unlike any military situation Leon had ever been in. He was in a convoy of very large military vehicles, almost the size of combine harvesters. It's like the Russian army, or something . . .

They were going down a dirt road. Leon was sitting some kind of deck portion of a gigantic armored personnel carrier, enjoying the sunshine with his M4 across his lap.

For some reason somebody was fussing about gas masks - "pro masks". Some admin guys, headquarters pukes, wanted everyone to make sure their gas masks fit . . . change out the filter, clean the things . . . they kept going on and on about gas masks . . .

Leon was thinking, 'Fuck a bunch of gas masks! NBC - Nuclear-Biological-Chemical - stands for "No Body Cares - right?'
Now the convoy was moving through a semi-built up area, buildings of bare cement in various states of decay on either side of the road. It reminded Leon of West Africa.

Then, things started to move fast, the street was filled with clouds and clouds of tear gas, thicker than fog. Then all of a sudden, there were these assholes emerging from the clouds of gas!

They're wearing gas masks of course - and business suits of all things - and they're armed with 12-gauge pump shotguns.

Suddenly the whole gas mask issue is very important!

Drowning Creek

Leon pulled his mask on faster than anybody in the entire history of NBC. The seal wasn't right around his chin so he caught a whiff of gas. He went ahead and did the overpressure and suction test, and the mask was on nice and tight.

Then Leon was at his position at the railing of the giant fighting vehicle he was riding on and they're shooting down these assholes in business suits. Shotgun balls are flying everywhere but at this range their rifles had the advantage and they were slaying them. Shooting them down like dogs in the street!

Leon jarred himself awake. 'What a fucked up dream,' he thought. Then he realized he could see stuff, without turning on his headlamp. A faint light glowed through the window directly above him. The wind still howled but not as much as before, and the slapping of the waves on the shell of the building seemed somehow less than before. Leon looked about his distorted surroundings, and noticed the kitchen counter and cabinets on the side of the wall. Leon scrambled down his pile of furniture entered the water, which was now waist deep, and made his way towards the wall with the counter and the cabinets. He scrambled up to the door which was now like a hatch in what was now the ceiling, turned the knob and pushed it open.

Hot, rain-filled but fresh air blasted him in the face. The sky overhead was gray, but over the black, angry sea a yellow glow gave Leon a burst of hope that he felt in his heart. Dawn. He'd managed to ride out the storm . . . he was still alive!

Peter Crittenden

* * *

There was choppy black water everywhere. Where before there had been streets and front yards was now completely inundated. Cars were stacked haphazardly up against houses, the flood's waves splashing against them. The storm was blowing itself out, but the flood of the storm surge had not yet abated.

'What a mess,' Leon thought.

The view across what used to be the beach to the churning seas beyond, was almost terrifying.

Black water, white capped waves churned up and crashed against the pier and all of the dwellings up and down the beachfront. Leon was amazed that a single thing remained in place, the destruction was not as widespread as he would have imagined, despite the storm surge's wave rolling over what was once dry land.

Leon estimated he could strike out, go look for the boat. Securing the device, and his phone, he looked about for a way to get off the building safely. He didn't dare jump into the water, not only because he didn't know its depth, but he had no idea what was beneath the surface. Be no good to survive a hurricane on the Outer Banks, have a building fall over with him inside, only to end up impaled on some kind of structural timber or something. He'd have to carefully climb down what had been the railings of wooden exterior stairs that joined the little decks, two levels up from the ground.

What had been the street was covered in brown water. Leon looked at the house across the street – the water appeared to be halfway up to the doorknob on the front door. *'About knee deep,'* Leon thought. Curtains of light rain still lashed the

Drowning Creek

waters, but not as strong as before and Leon figured he could make it back to the golf course, maybe find his boat.

If his boat wasn't there, he'd just turn around and go back to the beach house, wait for somebody to show up and give him a ride back to the mainland.

Leon hadn't counted on the current – the water in the street was deeper than what he'd estimated, looking at how far up it had come to the house across the street – and it was moving. '*Oh well, in for a penny, in for a pound,*' he thought. With that he leaned forward and moved on through the swirling brown water.

Trying to figure the way back was challenging now that water covered everything. Leon moved in a generally westerly direction, keeping the beach and the blowing storm to his back as he attempted to retrace his steps back to the golf course. A siren went off. Leon turned, looked over his shoulder. A fire truck was about a half a block away, a man hanging out the door on the running board.

"Hey!" the man hollered. "Hey you!"

Leon ignored him, turned and continued to plow on towards the golf course.

"HEY YOU!" The fire truck pulled up behind him. Leon turned.

"Yeah," he replied.

"Where do you think you're going?" the man asked.

"To the golf course," Leon replied.

"The golf course? What for?"

Peter Crittenden

"I thought I'd get a round in," Leon answered.

The man gave him an exasperated look. "Don't you know this place was under order for evacuation?" he said. "What are you doing here?"

"The storm is over," Leon said. "I'm going over to the docks, other side of the golf course. I parked my boat over there."

"You think it'll still be there?"

"I dunno. Gonna find out."

"What are you still doing here? The entire outer banks were supposed to be evacuated."

"I know. I wasn't here. I came over yesterday afternoon, in my boat."

"Mister, that's crazy."

"Yes, I know."

"What are you gonna do if your boat isn't there?"

"Come back and ask you for a ride back to the mainland."

The man made a gesture of exasperation with his free hand and climbed back into the fire truck. Leon turned and continued on his way.

The golf course was completely underwater, of course. It resembled more a lake than a golf course, or maybe a wide tropical river, punctuated with the funny little flags marking where the putting greens were. Leon tried to concentrate on his footing, aware that the sand bunkers now represented places where the water would be deeper than the hip-level waters he now waded through. He became aware of the first sand bunker when suddenly he was chest deep in the water.

Drowning Creek

Leon struggled across, keeping his phone and the device in his hands over his head.

He came to the other side of the submerged sand trap and had some difficulty gaining a footing on the turf. The water became shallower as he approached what a submerged putting green, from the proximity of the little flag with the numeral 7 on it. Then the water became deeper, back up to mid-thigh, and he moved on. An alligator came swimming by with a large dog carcass in its jaws.

"Hello, Mister Crocky-Gator," Leon said. "You go your way and I'll go mine." The large reptile ignored him.

Leon struggled through two more sand traps to where the water came up to his neck, moved across areas of varying depth until at last he could make out the docks. Lo and behold, there she was. "Oh, you beauty," Leon whispered. "You beautiful, beautiful boat."

The docks floated independent of their pilings, to go up and down with the tides, and his boat was still there, still securely moored to the dock. Leon looked at the sides of the boat carefully, it didn't even seem to be marked from rubbing up against the dock. He climbed aboard and marveled at his luck. Then he primed the fuel lines, turned the ignition and the engines fired right up. Time to go home.

The journey back across the sound was easier this time. It was full daylight and the storm was really dying down. The wind and the waves were behind him this time. With following seas, Leon easily made it across the sound. He steered towards the little marina at the gas station, secured the boat to its mooring, then walked – a little unsteady, but hardly worse for wear and tear, considering his ordeal – across the docks and to the convenience store.

Leon caught a glimpse of himself in the reflection on the glass front of the store. He looked like something the cat dragged in. When the guy behind the counter looked up, he looked like he'd seen a ghost.

"Hey," said Leon.

"You're BACK," the man practically gasped.

"Yeah."

There was a silence for a bit. "Your boat's back there," Leon nodded his head towards the marina. "She's fine." Then, "I gotta get a cup of coffee."

"Sure, Mister," the man said. "You want something to eat? I just put those dogs on." He pointed to the hot dog machine, the hot dogs rotating on their rollers.

"That'd be great," Leon said. "I'm starving to death."

Leon scarfed down a hot dog, washed it down with coffee, hot and black, then made himself another hot dog and poured himself another cup of coffee.

"Can I have my truck back?" he asked. "You can keep the thousand dollars."

"Uh, yeah, sure, Mister," the guy said.

"What do I owe you for the dogs and the coffee?"

"Don't worry about it, Mister," the guy said. "On the house. I'm just glad to see you made it back in one piece."

"Thanks," said Leon. "I'm gonna need to fill her up."

"Sure. Pump Six."

Leon glanced over to the pumps. "She's diesel," he said.

"Oh, right," the guy said. "Pump Seven. And don't worry about it," he added. "I'll take it out of the thousand."

"Thank you," Leon said. "You don't have to do that."

"I want to, Mister. I'm that damn glad to see you're alive."

"Thank you. Thank you very much." Country people are like that.

XVIII

It was already dark when Leon finally got home and pulled his truck back into his driveway. Nancy was waiting for him at the door. "Oh my God," she gasped, "You look like you've been through hell!"

"I have, but that was a long time ago," Leon quipped. "This wasn't so bad."

"Ewww!" Nancy recoiled from him. "You SMELL like you've been through Hell! The sewers of Hell!"

"Yeah," Leon admitted, "I need a shower."

"Just take your boots and your clothes off here, I'll get a laundry basket. Don't walk that stink through the house."

"Okay," Leon said. "I need a beer, also."

"I'll get you one. Go ahead and get in the shower."

The needles of hot water came down and loosened the tense muscles in his neck and shoulders. Leon closed his eyes and tilted his head back. Nancy came into the bathroom and handed him a cold beer. Then she undressed and joined him in the shower, and things got even better.

Later, after the shower and then a bite to eat, something occurred to Leon. "You study computer science and technology, right?"

"Right."

Drowning Creek

"Wait here, I have something I want to run past you." Leon went into the bedroom and retrieved the strange device. He placed it on the coffee table. "What is this?"

Nancy took hold of the cylindrical device and traced her finger along the inscriptions and the lines engraved along the metallic surface. Then she slid the sleeve back and revealed a row four disks inset within, with an empty space for one more.

"Oh my God," she gasped.

"What? What is it?"

"It's a," she started to say, "it appears to be a, well, it's a sort of a storage device. More a key, really."

"A key? What kind of a key?"

"A key for cryptocurrency. This is the sort of thing that people with crypto accounts - very large crypto accounts - use to access their accounts."

"Is that thing worth a lot of money?" Leon asked.

"Could be, but we have no way of knowing."

"Why not? We need a password or something?"

"Or something," Nancy replied. "It's missing a part, right here." She pointed to where the disks sat within the interior, to the empty slot.

"What does it do," Leon asked, "how does it work?"

"Well, it's called a key, a crypto key, but it's really like a bank book, combining an encrypted drive that accesses and unlocks the crypto account its associated with. It's like this; if you have a big account, like a corporate account, which several people – more than one at least – shares, these wheels here are each party's individual key. You need all five keys to access the account, but this is better than passwords or biodata, like fingerprints or iris scans,"

"I get it," Leon said, "Because passwords can be forgotten, fingers or eyes can be, you know, lopped off or gouged out or whatever, but this way as long as you have the wheels the account can be accessed."

"That's right," Nancy said. "So even if one of the members of the account dies, for example, all you need is their wheel. In this case, there are four wheels present."

"Does that mean there's a fifth wheel out there, somewhere?"

"Could be. Probably. Or it could be there are only four wheels – four members, that is – to this thing. The fifth wheel slot could be a spare, to add a future account holder, or to make the encryption more complex. Exponentially so."

"How would one know?"

"Get it near a computer that's connected to the Internet. It'll either open the account, or it won't. If it doesn't, then you need the fifth wheel."

"Can we try it and find out?"

"We can," Nancy said, "but two of three things are going to happen."

"What's that?"

"Either the four wheels will open the account and we will have access to the entire contents, or it will fail to open the account because it requires a fifth wheel."

"That's two things."

"Yes," Nancy continued. "The third thing that will happen is that whoever's associated with the account will become aware that somebody has used this device to open it, or to attempt to open it."

"Does that matter?"

"Probably – because whoever it is, they might lock the account."

"Is that likely?"

"I really don't think so – the whole concept of cryptocurrency is it's a stand-alone monetary value that belongs solely to the owner – that is, the person who sets up the account. Third parties, governments, collection agencies, etcetera, cannot access it. You can't put a lean on crypto like you can a bank account. Conceptually speaking, only the person who has this device – and all the wheels - can access this account."

"Let me see if I got this right," Leon said. "I've got this thing, this crypto key. And it may or may not be the key to an account of a significant amount of crypto."

"Oh, it certainly is," Nancy said, pointing to some numbers emerging on the little screen. "For one thing, it's loaded, it's not an empty account."

"And it may or may not be able to open the account and give me access."

"It either can or it cannot," Nancy said. "You might be able to do it with just the four wheels, or you might need the fifth wheel."

"Right. And in the process of finding out, the actual account owner would become aware that somebody's tinkering around with his or her crypto."

"Oh, they would become aware of that, for certain. They'd get a message in their crypto wallet, even if they can't open their account."

"Okay," Leon said, picking the device up. He slid the sleeve closed, replaced it into its little box and snapped it shut. "Thank you," he said. "You just gave me an education, and this thing is obviously a hot potato."

"Do you think this thing is why that guy rolled up here the other day and shot at you?"

"I'm beginning to think so, yes," Leon said. "That's about the only thing that makes sense, right now."

"I'd say so," Nancy agreed. "And I would advise you to hide it very well."

"That's what the turkey was all about," Leon said.

"Yes."

"I need to figure all this shit out," Leon moaned. "I need a plan."

"I'd say you need to find a new place to stash that thing and you need to find it sooner than later," Nancy said, "Because you're right – that thing is a total hot potato."

"You're right," said Leon. "You're absolutely right."

"Leon, tell me what's going on," Nancy said quietly.

Drowning Creek

Leo looked at Nancy for a moment while he contemplated how much he was going to tell her. For a moment he actually contemplated telling her some cock-and-bull story about being hired to do a private investigator gig for a suspicious wife or something. Then he realized it was time to lay it all out for her. And so he explained everything. Pulling Ivy out of the creek, Rudy, the situation with Gato, the No-Name gas station, the white vans, everything.

"Good Lord," Nancy exclaimed, "All this has been going on just over the past week or two, while you and me have been getting together?"

"Yes."

"You sure kept it pretty quiet," she said. "Talk about walls up."

Leon shrugged.

"And whatever is going on has something to do with the thing, the crypto key, right?" Nancy asked, her eyes narrowing.

"Maybe," Leon replied.

"And that guy who fired shots at you the other day? And those cops who showed up at the house? The guys you said were Feds?"

"Yes, actually."

"Wow," she said. "That's all I have to say. Wow."

* * *

"Consider this," Nancy suggested. "The human brain is deeper than the ocean. The brain can contain the entire Universe, all the stars and planets and the deep vastness of space. The brain is our most powerful tool, and when we can harness even ten percent of its power, humans can accomplish incredible, amazing things."

"Okay," Leon said. He liked what he was hearing.

She went on, "Now think about the subconscious mind. Our subconscious works continuously, while we are awake, and while we sleep."

"The subconscious mind never rests. It's always on duty because it controls our heartbeat, our breathing, all the vital processes and functions of the body. And," she paused for effect, "it knows the answers to all our problems."

Leon was listening intently now.

"What happens on our subconscious level influences what happens on our conscious level. In other words, what goes on internally, even unconsciously eventually becomes our reality. The subconscious mind will translate into its physical equivalent, by the most direct and practical method available.

"So, as a problem-solving technique, the goal is to direct your subconscious mind to create the outcomes you seek, to tap into your subconscious mind to unlock connections and solutions to whatever is the challenge at hand."

"Okay," Leon said, genuinely interested. "Where are you going with this?"

"Here's a simple routine that I do," Nancy said. "Ten minutes before going to sleep, I meditate on whatever it is I'm trying to accomplish, then write down my objectives.

"If I was you, I'd ask myself loads of questions related to that thing. I never go to sleep without making a request to my subconscious. While you're sleeping, the subconscious mind will get to work on those things.

"What happens after you awaken, immediately after sleep, the brain is most active and creative. The subconscious is loosely mind-wandering while we sleep, making contextual and temporal connections. Creativity is making connections between different parts of the brain.

"The last thing you want to do," Nancy said, looking into his eyes, "Is check your smartphone within the first few minutes after you wake up. It's such a distraction, such a drain on your creative energies. What I do is go to a quiet place, do some meditation and grab my journal.

"In my journal, I thought-dump for several minutes. This way, instead of focusing on input like most people who are checking their notifications, I focus on output. This is how I tap into higher realms of clarity, learning and creativity. It's like crystallized intelligence."

"This makes sense," Leon said. "Mental creativity always precedes any physical action. Before you do anything, you need a plan. Before a building is physically constructed, there's a blueprint."

"Exactly," Nancy said. "Your thoughts are the blueprint of the life you are building one day at a time. When you learn to channel your thinking – both consciously and subconsciously – you create the conditions that make the achievement of your goals inevitable.

"We are the designers of our destiny," Nancy concluded. "Tapping into your subconscious will help you crystallize where you want to go, and how you will get there."

XIX

On his way to the FBI field office downtown Raleigh, Leon first swung by Group HQ at Bragg, went into the Personnel office and dropped his retirement paperwork. Already burnt out and disgruntled, this entire affair with Haglin was the straw that broke the camel's back - he'd had enough reindeer games with the Army. *'Time to blow this popsicle stand.'* All Leon needed was a signature and that bought him three months of stored up retirement leave before he signed out of the Army - more than enough time to work on this business with Gato. Leon had heard of guys going on retirement leave and picking up overseas contracts while they were technically still on active duty. It isn't illegal to double dip like that but it is illegal to go into an overseas combat zone to do it. VERY illegal, but it happens.

* * *

"Okay," Kleckner said, nodding to the computer on a table over to the side. "Let's have a look at Eagle Eye. Let's see what we can see about this No-Name gas station."

Originally designed for pilots to familiarize themselves with close-in ground attack runs or landings at unfamiliar air strips, ground pounders like Infantry and Special Forces also find Eagle Eye useful as a sort of reconnaissance tool. If one wants a three-dimensional look at something from an oblique angle – a route, for example - it can hover over a road or a trail as the viewer moves along it, or around all four sides of a

Drowning Creek

building. If Eagle Eye doesn't have it stored, a drone is deployed to provide up-to-date imagery and footage, sometimes in real-time. It's like Google Earth combined with the photo sphere street view capability on Google maps. If it doesn't have a view of something or the angle one is looking for, it can cough one up pretty damn fast.

They pulled up some chairs around the monitor. McBride got the thing over to Deep River Road. There was the gas station, grass growing up through the cracks in the concrete. There was the convenience store. There were the four white vans parked perpendicular to the service bays.

"Zoom in."

McBride zoomed it. Four white vans. They trio leaned in. Something looked fishy about the roofs on those vans.

"Fly us around," Leon said.

The thing zoomed around. Now they could see the sides of the buildings, could see into the service bays, even with the vans parked in front of them, where they could get the angles to look over the vans. They could see the guys working on the vans – it was all still shots but practically real-time. The imagery was probably taken yesterday afternoon, or possibly earlier, that morning.

"What's going on with the roofs on those vans?" Kleckner asked.

"There are no roofs on those vans," McBride said. "It looks like they've cut them out."

McBride was right - the vans had big square cuts in their roofs. The guys – Gato's crew – were building something inside, with what looked like planks of wood - two-by-fours -

and large diameter pipes. White pipes, looked like PVC. And something else.

"Zoom in," Leon said. "On that van there. What are they doing to it?"

One of the guys was putting together what looked like a full-width, canvas, roll-back sunroof, like on one of those old Citroën bug-type cars. "It's like a sliding rag top," McBride suggested.

"Yeah, but what's with the pipes and the planks?" Kleckner asked. "Are they making taco trucks out of these things?"

"I'll tell you what's with the pipes and the planks," Leon said. "I've seen something like this before."

"What is it?" they both said at the same time. Jinx.

"If I told you," Leon answered, "You'll both think I was crazy. Hell, I think I'm crazy, just looking at this."

"What is it?" Double Jinx.

"It's a multiple launch mortar system."

"W-H-A-A-A-?-?-?"

"Homemade, improvised, but incredibly effective."

"What, how?" Kleckner asked.

"I've seen it in Colombia," Leon said. "The FARC used to fabricate them, used them as hip-pocket artillery. You've got like ten-inch diameter launch tubes that can launch projectiles. They used empty propane gas cylinders as shells. Propane is the main source of cooking fuel down there so there's plenty of empty gas cylinders, and the small cylinders make a perfect improvised artillery shell. They would fill them with an ammonium nitrate fertilizer explosive charge, and jellified gas, and nails or ball bearings, creating explosive, shrapnel-filled incendiary projectiles. Real nasty stuff. They're especially effective against area targets such as army bases, or airfields.

"Or football stadiums," McBride said.

"Or football stadiums," Leon acknowledged. "We had a lot of them in Arauca Province, up on the Venezuelan border. The airport next to our compound in Saravena was hit by these "cylinderos", got tore up bad. These Irish assholes - the IRA - taught them how to make them and taught them how to initiate them remotely, with cell phones. They would just park a vehicle somewhere, walk away, hit the numbers on their cell phone and it would launch. The system can lob these things about twelve hundred meters, which is three quarters of a mile. There were a couple of captured ones on the Colombian Army base in Saravena. To the naked eye, on street level, they just look like an ice cream truck, or a pickup truck with a large cooler on the back. But from overhead, we can see the cut-out on the roof, and the tubes which launch the projectiles."

"Is that what this is?"

"That's what it looks like."

"How accurate is this shit?"

"Very," Leon said. "They'd put together a system, then go out to a remote location and test fire it, to get the ballistics. Kind of like reverse-engineered gunnery – instead of knowing their charge and the trajectory, and calculating angle and deflection off that, they'd just fire the thing off and see where the rounds went. Then they'd know how far off the target to park the van for an effective attack. The IRA Provos used to do the same thing against British bases in Northern Ireland. That's where the FARC learned it from."

"You're going with a lot of supposition here," Kleckner said. "How do you know so much about this shit?"

"I'm a Green Beret, it's my job to know how my enemy thinks. In this particular case, Gato told me himself."

"GATO?"

"Yeah. He used to make these things. The IRA taught him, personally. He used to brag about shit like this to impress us."

"I dunno," Kleckner said. "Even a written statement from you on what you just said, that wouldn't be enough to get a warrant on these shitheads," Kleckner said. "No way any DA is going to go for a conviction, based on just what you just laid out."

"Look, I'm telling you we need to keep a close eye on these bastards," Leon said. "This is more than just a bunch of vans with lumber and PVC pipes and the roofs cut out. I'd like to see them stopped before they go operational, if possible, and send them up the river for like, forever. We're probably going to have to wait until they've put the whole thing together and go out somewhere to test fire their mortar systems and find their ballistics. And even then, this stuff is so simple it's basically just a giant potato gun. I mean, is it really illegal to make a homemade mortar and fire it off in a field?"

Kleckner and McBride looked at each other, and then at Leon.

"Not really," McBride said. "In America you can actually own a cannon. Don't even need a permit or anything."

Drowning Creek

"Yeah, but making explosive bombs to launch out of tubes has got to be another thing altogether," Leon said. "At some point or another these guys start breaking some serious laws."

"Yeah, but is it enough?" McBride asked. "We need something bigger than just these guys are gearing up for the ultimate Fourth of July fireworks display. How do we prove intent? We need to get these guys on conspiracy charges, terrorist charges. These guys need to be tried, convicted, thrown into Supermax and the key thrown away."

"Either that," Leon said, "or just plain killed outright."

"We can't just kill them," Kleckner observed.

"Well, sure we can," Leon said. "Terrorists need to be wiped out. That's the best way."

"That's illegal."

"That's an artificial constraint," Leon said, "but I get it, of course. There are rules of engagement, the law of the land, and we're bound by it. I was just saying."

"Of course."

"There's always self-defense, of course," Leon added, "or shot while trying to escape, but of course we don't talk about that."

"We can't even THINK about that," McBride said.

"Of course not," Leon replied.

"Of course not," Kleckner repeated.

"What do you envision here, as a start point?" McBride asked.

"Hey, you guys are the secret policemen, I'm just the knuckle dragging snake eater," Leon said. "What I'd like is for you guys to keep a close eye on them, now that I've given you an idea what it is they are up to, and determine when is the right time to swoop in and interdict these guys, before they go operational."

McBride made a noise like he was clearing his throat. "What," said Leon, dryly.

"We can't just go in and interdict these guys because we think there's a crime in progress," McBride said. "We're going to have to have some kind of hard evidence. For all we know, these guys are putting together super customized taco vans, and are about to go into business selling tacos at football games."

'*Lord Almighty*,' Leon thought, inwardly rolling his eyes. '*What's it gonna take to light a fire under people's asses?*'

XX

Everything sucked and nothing was going anywhere near the way Leon wanted things to be going. What he needed was a private army to do surveillance on the No-Name gas station, surveillance on Gato's house, a signals intercept team to monitor communications between Gato and his team, and a complete scan at the gas station and at Gato's house, for cameras, any kind of motion detectors or listening devices. Instead he had two things: Jack, and shit.

This should be the watch and wait phase, the most important and delicate phase of the hunt. Instead it was all wait and no watch and there was nothing Leon could do but kick back, be miserable, and enjoy his misery as he died of boredom.

* * *

Leon was standing on the roof of a beachside hotel. There was a railing around the edge of the building which was sort of like a cruise ship. Leon and Rudy were watching the waves roll in. These were huge rollers towering over them forty, fifty, sixty feet high. The waves were inundating the lower floors, and the spray was hitting Leon and Rudy, saturating them. It was like being in a car wash. "The waves cannot hit us here," Rudy stated flatly, "we are safe, holding on to the rail." Then the Big One came.

Peter Crittenden

It was enormous, the size of a mountain, dwarfing the hotel. The wave was covered in flotsam, debris sucked out to sea from earlier waves, to where it looked like an actual hillside covered in vegetation. It was obvious to Leon and Rudy they had to get the hell out of there, so they made their way downstairs, and as they did they passed these enormous windows and it was like looking through the glass at the Monterey Bay Aquarium, only instead of clear water and exotic fish they saw brown water with debris floating in it, going up and down.

Out in front of the hotel Leon and Rudy found themselves in a Southeast Asian marketplace. Produce stacked on tables with colorful plastic tablecloths beneath wide umbrellas and awnings. The dirt street was dry, the enormous wave had not brought the sea here, for some reason. There was a small Italian sports car, open with no roof. Leon commandeered it. What else it didn't have was a brake pedal, only an accelerator and a clutch. 'Oh well, I'll manage,' Leon thought, 'If you know what you're doing, all you really need is an accelerator and a clutch.' Leon and Rudy climbed in. It was a tight fit.

But it was obviously market day, the plaza was jam packed full of tables, baskets full of fruits and vegetables, fishermen's nets were draped off the columns and archways of the rustic buildings with their terra cotta roof tiles. Leon drove around and around but as he struggled to manipulate the controls of the tiny Italian sports car there was no way he could get out of the plaza. Then he noticed two men coming up behind him, they were wearing some kind of traditional Burmese costumes with big blousy sleeves, leather vests with straps and buckles all over them, and weird pillbox caps. The two men were wielding huge, curved swords and it was then that Leon noticed the heads, decapitated heads all around the place, on the market tables, all lined up along the top of a low wall, blood dripping down seeping into the dirt road.

Heads, heads, heads with contorted expressions on their faces attesting to their gruesome deaths. Absolutely horrific. Suddenly Leon found a way to get the tiny sportscar out of there so he turned that way. There was a big water puddle in the middle of the road but as he drove through it, he found it was not a puddle but a deep sink hole. The front tires went in and now they were stuck, there was no escape. Leon could not even get out of the sports car to make a run for it, the machine now held him in some sort of constraint, like a mechanical crab claw. The place was full of chopped off heads, and the men were now beside the car, looking down at Leon and brandishing their swords.

Unexpectedly, Rudy climbed over Leon, reaching out to the swordsmen, his face a mask of rage, his arms outstretch, hands grasping towards them. "YOU MOTHER FUCKERS!" he hollered. "I'M GONNA KILL YOU! I'M GONNA FUCK YOU UP!" The swordsmen's eyes grew wide and they

Peter Crittenden

instinctively took a step back as Rudy clambered over Leon and out of the car.

Next thing, bullets were hitting the sports car. Leon slunk down in a desperate attempt to make himself smaller than the tiny car. Coming down the block were about twenty drunk Burmese soldiers firing all over the place. Leon thought, 'Here I am going to die in a stupid dinky sportscar in some nameless market wearing a T shirt, shorts and flip flops. Not too gallant for a warrior.' One of the swordsmen made a run for it and was shot dead in the street. Leon thought the safest place to be with drunken Burmese shooting at them was directly behind the other sword guy, so he stepped out and became sandwiched between the swordsman to his front, Rudy stuck to his back. The Burmese came up and one of the drunk ones was yelling and trying to stick his rifle around the sword guy to shoot Leon and Rudy, the four of them doing a crazy dance going round and round in the street. An officer appeared firing his pistol in the air and yelling for everyone to stop. Then a stake bed truck appeared with more heads stuck on the stakes with another officer standing in the back yelling on a loudspeaker. A crazed Burmese raked the truck with automatic fire and killed the officer. Leon was thinking, 'This is MADNESS.'

Leon woke up in a cold sweat, gasping. Both his hands were white knuckle gripping the sheets.

"What is it honey? What is it?" Nancy moved to him.

"Nuthin'," Leon panted. "Bad dream."

"You were shouting out something. 'Heads, the heads!' Was it Iraq?"

"No."

"Afghanistan?"

"No."

"Then what?"

"Frikkin Burma."

"What?"

"Burma. That's where I saw the heads. There were heads all around the place. They were even driving trucks around with heads on stakes. Frikkin' Burma, of all places."

"What in the world were you doing in Burma?"

"They had a coup, it was a bloody mess. We had to go in and get the US citizens out, and there were these trucks driving around with heads on stakes."

"Why were you dreaming about that place?"

"I dunno. That was over twenty years ago. Haven't thought about that place in decades. Literally."

* * *

Leon and Nancy were lying together, naked in bed.

Peter Crittenden

"So who do you think killed Kennedy? Do you think the CIA did it?" Leon asked.

"I think there's a lot of disinformation floating around about that," Nancy replied, "and a whole lot of deliberately planted misinformation, and I certainly believe that what the Warren Commission came up with is flawed, but I don't think the CIA did it."

"Why? Or rather, why not?"

"Just think for a minute," she said, "If the CIA did it, if there was a conspiracy within the CIA to assassinate the President of the United States and make it look like somebody else did it, just think of all the moving parts that would have to be involved. It would require about a thousand operators and support personnel to pull off an operation like that. How do you keep all those people's mouths shut for all these years? Sooner or later someone gets religion, or gets disgruntled, or talks on their deathbed. It's been sixty years and not a peep. If there was a conspiracy, it wasn't from within this country."

"Then, who?" Leon asked.

"Most likely the Cubans, that's my hypothesis."

"The Cubans? Why?"

"Castro certainly had the motive – the CIA had conducted at least, what, fifty assassination attempts on his life."

"Really?"

"Yes, this is fully documented."

Drowning Creek

"But Oswald was hanging out with right-wing Cubans, down in New Orleans," Leon frowned.

"That, if anything, had to have been a deception operation," Nancy replied. "Oswald was a hard-core Communist. If those right-wing Cubans had any idea who he was, they would have kicked his ass and thrown him to the curb.

"To fully get it, we gotta back up a bit," she continued. "Oswald was a Communist, he'd defected to the Soviet Union. They didn't want him over there, apparently, they figured he was basically a mouth breather, not a lot of gray matter up there between the ears, so they shipped him off to Minsk to work in a factory, assembling televisions.

"In Minsk, Oswald meets up with Marina, daughter or niece of a KGB colonel, and he's making ten times more than the average factory worker at that time, and they put him up in a nice apartment which would normally have required, like, a ten-year waiting period to get into.

"But life in the Worker's Paradise wasn't what Oswald imagined, there weren't any bowling alleys or ice cream parlors out in Minsk, so he comes back to the States, with Marina and their newly born daughter in tow, and they settle in Dallas. If settle is a word you can apply to anything Oswald ever did. Oswald finds time to go down to Mexico City where he approaches the Soviet embassy.

"The Soviets didn't want anything to do with Oswald – they already knew he was a loon and were glad to be rid of him. That, and they rightly assess he's a hot potato, being watched by the CIA, which apparently turned out to be the case. They don't even let him in, they send him down the street to the

Cuban embassy, tell him maybe the Cubans got something for him. Nobody knows what transpired between Oswald and the Cubans, but we know Oswald was in New Orleans handing out Marxist literature, supporting the Fair Play for Cuba Committee – a pro-Castro organization."

"Right," Leon said. "But what about the far-right Cuban reactionaries Oswald was hanging out with in New Orleans? Oswald was even talking to small groups of Cuban refugees in Dallas."

"That had to be a deception operation," Nancy went on. "Remember, every intelligence operation has a deception plan, to mask it, to make it appear it is something it is not. This suggests there was some kind of conspiracy, and that the Castro regime was a likely culprit, right?"

"Uh, right," Leon replied.

"Right. Now this is where that theory falls apart: Oswald didn't go down to Mexico and meet with the Cubans until several months after his activities in New Orleans. That's sort of like the chicken coming before the egg. He didn't get the job at the Texas School Book Depository - which was on the President's motorcade route - until after he had returned to Texas from Mexico, a little over a month before the shooting on November 22 - but the route itself was not announced until only a few days before JFK's arrival in Dallas. How would Oswald – or any conspirators – have known to place him there, in order to frame him for the assassination – when nobody know what the President's route would be?

"There's a million angles to the Kennedy assassination conspiracy theories and under close inspection they all fall through your fingers like water. At the end of the day, that's what's wrong with all these crazy conspiracy theories. Like I said, sooner or later somebody's gonna talk, and in sixty years not a soul has had a come-to-Jesus moment. For an operation the size of which would require hundreds if not thousands of moving parts, that is simply not possible. Somebody would have talked. Hell, somebody would have spoken up in advance and said, 'Wait a minute, we're doing what? We're going to kill the President of the United States? Are you guys crazy?' It's just not possible."

Leon looked at Nancy and contemplated what she had just told him. Finally he spoke. "Wow. I never thought in a million years all that would be going on in the mind of a stripper."

"Asshole!" Nancy exclaimed with a laugh, mock punching his arm.

XXI

Leon's phone rang. It was Johnson, the CID guy. "Yeah," Leon grunted.

"Leon, what are you doing?"

"I'm hanging out at my crib. What are you doing?"

"There's some bad news, I just wanted to make sure you weren't driving."

"What's going on?"

"Haglin's dead."

"W-H-A-A-A-?-?-?" Leon nearly dropped his phone. "What happened?"

"Suicide," Johnson said. "He shot himself in the head with his shotgun."

"No way," Leon replied.

"Way."

There was no possible way Haglin shot himself in the head, Leon thought. He knew the man – suicide was simply not an option. "Where are you now?" he asked.

"I'm at Haglin's," Johnson answered.

Drowning Creek

"Wait for me, I'm coming over."

"Don't come over," Johnson said. "It's a crime scene, there's an active investigation going on. You can't come over."

"Sounds like you've already solved it. Fuck that, I'm coming over," Leon said.

Leon parked in the street in front of Haglin's place. The door was open and there was yellow CRIME SCENE tape was all over the place. The coroner's vehicle was parked in the driveway, halfway out onto the street and two guys from the morgue were lifting a gurney with a body bag into the back – obviously Haglin. Leon felt a sinking feeling in the pit of his stomach.

The only other cars around the place were Haglin's truck and a white Ford sedan with government plates. Leon came up to the door. "Hello?"

Johnson appeared at the door. "Hey."

Leon glanced inside, saw blood and brains splattered all over the wall where Haglin had obviously been sitting when he blew his brains out. *'IF he blew his brains out,'* Leon thought.

"Stay outside," Johnson said.

Leon glared at him as he shoved his way in. Johnson rolled his eyes. "Okay, just don't touch anything."

The place smelled like blood and brains. "Whaddya got?"

Johnson pointed to the shotgun, and the items from a gun cleaning kit on the floor around it. "He was obviously going to clean his shotgun and failed to clear it, first."

"No way," said Leon. "No fucking way."

"Why do you say that?"

"I knew Haglin, like I told you. We served on the same team for over two years, went everywhere, did everything together. I've known guys who've committed sideways and when they did, it never surprised me – you could see it, looking back. Haglin was not that way. He wasn't crazy and he wasn't depressed. He was as normal and rock solid as anyone I've ever known.

"Furthermore, we have a policy in Special Forces - treat all guns as if they are loaded always, and always, always, ALWAYS the first thing you do when you handle a weapon is you clear it. It's something we do religiously in Special Forces, something that's enforced and driven into the skulls of every single soldier on every single team I've ever served on. We operate out of tight quarters – team rooms, squad bays, houses - and everybody's armed to the teeth – we do everything, take every measure to preclude a negligent discharge. The fastest way to get kicked off a team is leave a loaded weapon anywhere beyond arm's reach. If a gun is not in use, if it's stored somewhere, it is unloaded first, and the first thing you do when you pick it up is make sure it's unloaded. Somebody did this to him," Leon concluded.

"Murder? You're sure about that?"

"You sure it ISN'T murder?"

Drowning Creek

"Go on."

"Look at it this way - if Haglin didn't kill himself – and I'm saying he didn't – then what happened was somebody came to the door, poked a gun in his face, sat him down and tied him up or used duct tape or zip ties to restrain him, then put a shotgun in his mouth and blew his head off. Then the murderer threw the shotgun on the floor, and laid out the cleaning kit, and then untied Haglin so when whoever found him, it looks like an accident." Leon continued, "Did you check the shotgun, or any of the cleaning kit items for prints?"

"For prints? No, why should we? Who's prints are we looking for, anyway? We're looking at it as a suicide and this is Haglin's shotgun."

"How do you know this is his shotgun? Did you even run the numbers on it? Look, if you're right and I'm wrong, Haglin's prints will be all over the shotgun, the cleaning kit and the ammo – maybe even the spent shell, I don't know if a print can hold up to what happens in the chamber when you fire a shotgun.

"But if I'm right and you're wrong, then you're going to find no prints or somebody else's prints on the shotgun. The numbers might tell you a story about where that shotgun came from – like, is it a stolen weapon from Baltimore or some shit. Then have the coroner look at Haglin's wrists for any sign of duct tape or zip tie restraints, string or rope, even. Haglin has one of those do-it-yourself security systems, accessed by his computer and/or phone. Have you looked at any of the camera footage?"

"No. We don't have the password on Haglin's computer to check his security camera footage."

"A password's going to slow you down? I thought you guys were shit hot. Where's Haglin's laptop?"

Silence.

"You've got Haglin's laptop, right?"

More silence.

"I mean, you were doing an investigation, right? You had his laptop and his phone, from before, right? I thought it was evidence – the laptop and his phone – and you guys had your hands on it, from right after you arrested him and sent him to the brig. You search the place?"

"Well, yeah."

"So his laptop's missing? Hmmm. Well if you don't know where it is, and I sure as hell don't know where it is, then somebody lifted it. Which means somebody was here before you got here, and if that somebody was the person who killed Haglin, they stole the laptop to preclude any access to the security cameras. Hell, I bet they stole his fucking phone. Is his phone anywhere around here?"

More silence.

"Sheesh," Leon exclaimed. "Have you looked at any footage from any of the other homes security systems in the neighborhood?"

"No, what would that tell us?"

Drowning Creek

"I tell you what," Leon said, looking Johnson dead in the eye, "If a white van pulled into this neighborhood in the last twelve hours or so, and was around longer than thirty minutes before it pulled out, then you and I both know who did this."

"You're dead certain Haglin didn't kill himself," Johnson stated.

"Why would he?" Leon asked. "Haglin was on his way to clearing his name, and yes he was kind of despondent about the whole thing with Ivy, but the incident here does not suggest a suicide - the cleaning kit makes it look like an accident with a firearm – an accident, not a suicide – and I'm saying it is an accident that did not happen. And there's something else."

"What?"

"If I'm right, and it wasn't an accident, and if you-know-who is behind this thing, then the whole plot thickens and better yet, we've got a way to scoop up Gato. Maybe his whole crew."

"Okay," Johnson said, "I'll call the sheriff's department, have them send over their prints guy, dust everything here."

"Good," said Leon, "Now then, does Caulfield or Aldridge know about this? Your buddies over at the Bureau know anything about this?"

"I dunno," said Johnson.

"You guys seriously do not talk to each other?" Leon asked, incredulous. "Well, they're going to want to know about this."

Peter Crittenden

'Am I the only guy with any sense of urgency on this thing?' Leon asked himself, for what seemed like the thousandth time. "Now let's go knocking on doors, see if the neighbors have any cameras that catch a view of the street."

The first door they knocked on, the guy who answered was the same guy who'd come up on Leon with a gun when Leon first came to Haglin's place, the day after finding Ivy in the creek. "Yeah, I was wondering about all the commotion," he said. Then when they told him, "Oh my God, that's terrible!" and, "Yes, sure, come in, I'll show you what I got on camera."

Sure enough, the camera he had looking over his driveway caught a corner of Haglin's property, and the street beyond. "Back up the vid," Leon said. "Past twenty-four hours."

There it was – a white van rolled in and parked right in front of Haglin's place. Leon looked at Johnson. Johnson didn't say a word.

* * *

Back inside Haglin's place, Leon looked at a framed quote on the wall:

> *"Men, Special Forces is a mistress. Your wives will envy her, because she will have your hearts. Your wives will be jealous of her because of her power to pull you away.*
>
> *This mistress will show you things never before seen and you will experience things that you have never before felt. She will love you, but only a little, seduce you to want more, to give more, and to die for her.*

Drowning Creek

She will take you away from the ones you love, and you will hate her for it, but leave her you never will. But if you must, you will miss her, or she is a part of you that will never be returned intact.

And in the end she will leave you for a younger man."

- James R. Ward, OSS

It occurred to Leon that Haglin would have been a whole lot hell better off if he'd just shacked up with Ivy, just like everybody else did. Instead, he went all out and married her. Ivy wasn't the kind of woman you're supposed to marry.

Kleckner and McBride, the FBI guys, should have been part of the conversation he just had with Johnson. Leon pulled out his card and gave Kleckner a call.

"Special Agent Kleckner," the voice on the other end said.

"Hey, this is Leon."

"What's up?"

"I'm at Haglin's place. Why aren't you here?"

"Yeah, we heard he shot himself. That kind of wraps up the case as far as we're concerned."

"What?" Leon exclaimed.

"It's a suicide, that's not a Federal crime," Kleckner said dryly. "The Bureau's business here is finished. We've got a caseload of other shit to take care of and we're moving on."

"But what about Gato and his band of merry men?" Leon asked.

"Listen, Leon, I'll tell it to you straight because you're a straight shooter," Kleckner replied. "That whole thing is a pipedream you're chasing, and we really don't have the resources to investigate every rabbit hole you crazy snake eaters want to jump down into."

"That's it? Case closed? *ARE YOU SHITTING ME???*" Leon was shouting into his phone.

"It was nice working with you, Leon," Kleckner said dryly. "Goodbye."

Click.

* * *

The shit was stacking up too high, too thick and too fast. As Leon walked out of Haglin's place, a little voice in his head told him to have a look under his truck - like the bomb checks they'd do, working overseas in the bad countries. Leon had long ago learned to listen to that little voice, and so he got down on his back and scooted under his truck.

Bingo – there it was, bigger than Stuttgart - a black plastic box, the size of a cigar box, stuck to his frame with magnets. Leon figured it wasn't a bomb, because if it was, why hadn't it gone off already, before he got to Rudy's place? Anyway – why kill him, if they possibly suspect he's got something they want? Leon pulled the black box off, rolled out from under his truck and inspected it. It was a plastic box with snap closures, like a gun box or any kind of plastic box used to store delicate equipment. He opened it. A big blue square shaped battery occupied two thirds of the box, wired into an electronic circuit board, which in turn was wired into a cellphone.

A cellphone tracker. '*Bastards*!' He figured it wasn't the Feds, because they would have used the two thousand dollar model, not this do-it-yourself Brand X version. This was obviously Gato's crew.

Leon glanced around – time to have some fun. There were several cop cars up and down the street, one right in front of his truck. Walking around the front of his truck, Leon dropped to his knee, pretending to tie his shoe. Then he dropped and rolled onto his back, reached under the cop car and placed the box to the exterior of the spare tire well, where it was obscured by the trunk. '*Let the bastards have some fun with that.*'

XXII

Leon and Nancy were sitting out back of his place, by the pool. Hovering in the air about six feet away from their faces was a small four propellor drone, which Nancy was controlling via a device that featured two joysticks she manipulated with her thumbs and a small tablet which provided a visual interface.

"Okay, show me what you can do with this cool toy," Leon said.

"Men and toys," Nancy said. "Pay attention, I'll show you what this thing can do, so even you can operate it, Cave Man." Leon rolled his eyes at this, "Now look," she indicated the tablet screen, where the video depicted themselves, as seen by the drone.

"The remote controller outputs a live video feed via HDMI to the capture card," Nancy explained. "The capture card receives the input data and transmits it to the laptop for encoding. The streaming software will take over encoding the video for streaming."

"Okay," said Leon. "I get that. The tricky part is how do we keep the drone surreptitious?"

Nancy went on, "This drone can go about three hundred feet up in the air but that's it – it's not a military grade, full size drone that can hover at altitudes of up to ten thousand feet where no one can see it. The trick with this thing is not to let it stand out against a blue sky, or a dark background like a stand of pine trees. It's white so it can potentially hide in an overcast sky."

"Right. Too bad it isn't German Field Grey."

Nancy manipulated the joysticks and the drone gained altitude. The view on the laptop screen depicted the porch where they sat, then the entire back of the house and the pool area, then half of the neighbors' backyard and their deck. They could even see through the sliding glass doors into the neighbors' house. "Oh look," said Nancy, "they're walking around naked!"

"Yes, they're nudists," Leon said. "They have naked pool parties in the summertime."

Nancy looked around. "Can we have naked pool parties?" she asked.

"Bring some of your friends from work," Leon replied, "and we can have full blown Roman orgies."

"Is that what you want?"

"Let's focus on the task at hand," Leon said. "Right now we want to look at some clowns I think are up to no good, bona fide bad guys. Play time comes later. When the weather warms up."

Nancy smiled at this.

Leon looked up in the air at the drone. It was hovering silently about a hundred and fifty feet above them, almost invisible against an overcast sky.

"What are the legalities here?" Leon asked.

"In North Carolina, it's illegal use a drone for surveillance of a person or private property," Nancy replied.

"Okay. I guess I just want to know what laws I'm breaking, how and when," Leon said.

"FAA drone regulations require that drones must be under fifty-five pounds," Nancy said.

"I think we're well within that," Leon said.

"And operators must keep the drone in sight at all times," Nancy continued, "which is sort of a self-enforcing law, because of the signals capabilities on these."

"We'll try to keep within the spirit of the law," Leon said. "Not that it matters much," he went on. "We're breaking the law anyway, using it for surveillance."

"Yes," Nancy acknowledged.

Nancy hovered the drone to where it was directly over the roof, looking obliquely into the neighbor's yard. "Now we can barely see the thing, and the neighbors can't see it at all. Theoretically, at least."

"Yeah, but now we can't see the neighbors," Leon said.

"Well, at least we're back into legal space," Nancy said. "Well, now you know the capabilities and limitations of this thing. Do you want to fly it?"

"Sure," Leon said, taking the controller. The view on the screen zoomed way out as Leon lost control of the device, then stabilized as he brought it to a hover and slowly brought it back down to lower altitude. "Other than keeping the thing stealthy, what are the challenges?"

"There might be a problem with battery life," Nancy remarked.

"What can we do about that?" Leon asked.

"Not much," Nancy admitted. "After a certain period of time – about fifteen or thirty minutes – the drone has to come down to recharge it's batteries."

"What if we have more than one drone?" Leon asked. "Swap 'em out?"

"That would work."

"Okay," said Leon. "Then, because two is one and one is none, we'll have three drones. That way we'll have seamless coverage. One is up while two are being recharged."

"We can even run them all off the same controller," Nancy said. "Just have dedicated channels."

"Okay," said Leon. "What about counter electronics? Can the bad guys detect that they're being spied upon?"

"Yes and no," said Nancy. "A drone's transmitter and receiver communicate via radio signals. Radio frequency sensors can capture and track different pieces of information, including drone make, model, serial number, drone's current location, even the location of the pilot as far as 100 miles, given weather conditions and terrain."

"So we can hide out using terrain masking?"

"Theoretically, yes," Nancy said. "But there's a more effective way. Simply spoof the signal, so that any radio frequency detector out there thinks they're just picking up the signal coming from, say, a UPS van, or even somebody's smart refrigerator.

"Refrigerator?" Leon asked, incredulous.

"Yes," Nancy replied. "People have fridges nowadays that are connected to the cloud and send text messages to their phones, tell them all kinds of things, such as what's inside, calendar entries, even alerts if the refrigerator's door is left open."

"So if the bad guys have any kind of detection capability, we can simply mask our signal signature as somebody's fridge?"

"Yes," said Nancy, "We can do that, and it's not difficult. Especially if we're using several drones, because multiple radio signals aren't easy to detect using RF technology."

Leon considered what he'd just learned. Next on the agenda was a little trip up to the No-name – he'd have to borrow one of the cars from his buddy at the car rental agency, couldn't risk showing up in his truck. Time to do a bit of drone piloting, take some pictures.

XXIII

Haglin's wake was at the Irish pub in Southern Pines, a quaint, traditional southern town surrounded by old growth pine forests that is on the opposite side of Fort Bragg from the unregulated sprawl and hustle and bustle of Fayetteville. Southern Pines is almost an hours' drive west of Fort Bragg, and culturally it is light years away from Fayetteville.

In earlier times the Irish pub was the old fire station. At some point in the Seventies it was converted to a pub, and over time it became a notorious Special Forces hangout.

The thing was going in full swing when Leon got there. Leon went to the part of the bar near the entrance where the cash register was, where he could stand on the steps overlooking the crowd, got the bartender's attention and put a couple hundred-dollar bills down on the top of the cash register, then he rang the bell.

"Gentlemen!" he called out. The room fell silent. "Most of y'all knew Rudy Haglin, and most of y'all know me, but none of you knew Rudy like I knew Rudy, 'specially what's been going down this past few weeks. This round is on me."

There was a pause, and then one of the guys at the far end of the bar lifted his glass. "Here's to Rudy," Leon stated, simply. Everybody else lifted their glasses, and Leon picked up the glass of whiskey the bartender had just placed in front of him.

Some of the guys said "'Till Valhalla," and a lot of the guys repeated "'Till Valhalla." It's something Green Berets utter when speaking of fallen comrades, or even those who died by their own hand, for even though the Viking Paradise is reserved for warriors who die in battle, a soldiers' suicide may be considered a long-term, residual effect of combat.

'How ironic,' Leon thought grimly. *'I'm the only one in the room that knows that Rudy actually did die at the hands of the enemy. If there really is a Valhalla, that's where he is now.'*

Leon wasn't the only one who'd dropped some coin on the bar that night. It's an old military tradition – people toss a pile of money in a bowl or in an upturned cowboy hat on the bar. It more than pays for the party and generously tips the staff, and there's a sizeable amount left that goes to the widow and kids of the fallen warrior. Of course, in Haglin's case there was no widow and there were no kids.

Leon worked his way to the end of the bar where an old friend greeted him with a handshake and a bear hug. "Good to see you, Dennis."

"Good to see you, Leon," Dennis replied.

"Is Charlie here?"

"Charlie is here, he's over there." Leon looked over, caught Charlie's eye, circled his finger in the air – hand-and-arm signal for rally point, or bring it in over here.

"What about Steve?" Leon asked.

"Steve's here too," Dennis said, "There he is, over there." Leon looked over to where Dennis indicated, caught Steve's eye, did the same gesture. Steve and Charlie made their way through the crowd to where Leon and Dennis were.

Drowning Creek

"What's up, brother?" Steve asked.

"Whaddya know?" Charlie asked.

"I've got some shit to tell you guys, some real heavy shit, and I can't tell it here, right now," Leon said. "But what I can tell you is Rudy didn't kill himself."

"Wha-a-a-a?" Dennis exclaimed.

"That's good to know," Steve said. "I guess. How do you know it?"

"I know it, and I'll tell you about it," Leon said, "But we can't really talk here. This is what I can tell you – Rudy didn't blow his head off with his shotgun, but I know who did it and why."

"That's some pretty heavy shit, bro," Dennis said. Then, to the bartender, "Hey Joe, can we use the upstairs room for a bit?"

"How long's a bit?"

"About thirty, maybe forty-five minutes," Leon said. "We got to talk something over."

"Okay," said Joe. "I'll get you the key."

"Get us a bottle of Irish whiskey while you're at it," Leon added.

"I've got Bushmills," Joe said.

"That's the stuff I like," Leon replied. "Thanks."

The team went upstairs.

The upstairs room was a card playing room. Leon had seen some pretty big pots go down in this place – more than ten times what he'd just placed on the bar downstairs. The men huddled around the table. Steve poured out four glasses of whiskey. "Okay, Leon, whaddya got?"

Leon told them the whole thing, starting with Ivy's death, then what Rudy had told him, how Ivy had gone nuts when she saw the photos from the private investigator Rudy had hired, and then he added his own conclusions. For brevity's sake, Leon left out the bit about the device and his trip out to the Outer Banks, so as not to muddy the waters too much while he was trying to explain everything.

"That fucking Gato freak is mixed up in this shit with Rudy?" Charlie exclaimed.

"Yeah," Leon confirmed.

"What the fuck do you think was going on? Ivy tried to kill Rudy because he busted her out, making it with Gato on the side?"

"I don't think Ivy was making it with Gato, that's not enough to turn on her husband and go ballistic like that, try to kill him. That's not the way it works when a spouse is caught playing around. It's certainly not how a woman responds."

"You'd never know with Ivy," Steve suggested.

"Maybe, maybe not, but not likely," Leon replied. And then Leon told them about Gato and his Iranian sidekicks, and the No-Name gas station, and of course how and why he thought Gato had killed Haglin.

"What the fuck are they up to?" Steve asked.

Leon laid out what he knew about the white vans, explained about his cooperation with the CID, the FBI, everything. Then he showed them the pics – copies of the black-and-white

Drowning Creek

glossies from Rudy's house, pics he'd taken with his drone, there were even pictures of Gato's crew – the Iranians - walking in and out of the house.

"There are four, maybe five white vans associated with these bozos at the No-Name gas station," Leon explained, laying out the overhead photos from his drone. "As you can see, they have been working on them, modifying them." Leon pointed out the cutout roofs, and the tubes arrayed in the inside of each van. "What's that look like?" he asked.

The guys peered over the photos. "You know," Charlie said, "that looks just like those improvised mortar systems the FARC used to do attacks on army bases and police stations, back in the day."

"That's exactly what I'm thinkin'," Leon said.

"Shit," Dennis said. "It's that same fucking system the narco-terrorists used down in Medellin. That shit they learned from the IRA."

"That's right," Leon confirmed. Then he told them about the football stadium.

"That's where the Army-Navy Game is being played, this weekend," Charlie said.

"Yep," Leon said. "Now put two and two together."

There was a momentary silence around the card table. Steve spoke up first. "You really think Gato is putting together some kind of monumental terrorist hit on a football stadium? The Army-Navy game? That's pretty fantastic, isn't it?"

"You guys are all trained in guerrilla warfare," Leon came back with. "What do you think?"

"Let me play Devil's advocate for a minute," Dennis said. "Maybe if you're a hammer the whole world looks like a nail. We're trained in guerrilla warfare, yes, and so we look at the whole world as if it's some sort of unconventional, guerrilla battlefield."

Chuck looked at Dennis. "It's not?"

"Ha, ha," Dennis laughed, with sarcasm. "What I'm saying is, you just might be leaning so far into this thing, Leon. Maybe you're seeing shit that isn't there. I mean, anybody's capable of bamboozling themselves."

Leon spoke up. "Your point is valid, Dennis, but there's another saying: if it looks like a duck, swims like a duck and it quacks like a duck, it's probably a duck. I personally believe Gato is an America-hating Communist from a long way back – so there's motive, right there – he knows how to do what I'm suggesting he's doing – there's method – and he's got the crew and capabilities to do it."

"Okay," Dennis interjected, "Have you spoken to anybody about this? Anybody besides us, that is. Does law enforcement, or maybe the Feds know anything about what you're telling us, here?"

"I told them," Leon said. "I told everybody everything I know. Hell, I've been talking to working with CID ever since I fished Ivy out of the creek." Leon continued, "Hell, they considered me a suspect, at first. Then they suggested I was making all this shit up, to get Rudy off the hook."

"Typical CID line of thought," Charlie observed.

"Yeah, no shit," Leon replied.

"Who exactly have you spoken to?" Charlie asked.

Drowning Creek

"CID was talking to me, like I said, working with me on this thing as long as there was an investigation. They even handed me off to CI and to the Feds - the Bureau." This caught the group's attention. "Yes, I know," Leon said. "Trouble is, I can't get anyone to pay any serious attention to what I'm saying. They keep playing me off like I'm some sort of crazy Green Beret. The whole Rambo syndrome."

"You ARE some sort of crazy Green Beret," Steve pointed out.

"That sure sounds funny coming from you, Steve," Leon shot back. "You still doing 'shrooms?"

"You know it bro," Steve grinned, "That's what's keeping me sane."

"Whatever floats yer boat," Leon replied. He went on, "Early on I was thinking this thing is going big, Jurassic Park big, and I told them everything I knew, everything I'd learned, and that I was interested in working with them. All I got back from everybody was 'Talk to the hand'. Especially after Rudy got killed."

"Killed?" Dennis remarked.

"Killed," Leon stated flatly. "That was no suicide. Leon was murdered, and Gato probably killed him personally. But nobody's looking at it like that. As far as law enforcement are concerned, it's a suicide, end of story. Me, I think it was a murder, I think Gato did it, and I think this is the reason why," Leon put his finger down on the photos of the white vans, laid out all over the table.

"So what are you going to do about all this?" Steve asked, indicating the photos on the table.

Peter Crittenden

"Well, I've been working with the authorities, I told them everything I told you guys and these pics prove what I'm saying is legit, but nobody's listening to me. I'm not getting any help or cooperation from the anybody," Leon said, "and I'm not looking forward to taking on Gato and his terrorist army singlehandedly. But knowing what I know, and considering what Gato did to Rudy, I gotta do something.

"Here's what the Feds don't know," Leon continued. "Just like you guys, I've got an insight into Gato's world and we all know others who have gone that route, earning tons of money for doing very little work, and that's what I think Ivy was doing. She was moving around in that world. Think about it, there's a ton of money floating around out there in narco-terrorist circles and Ivy loved the smell of that stuff. Gato had Ivy all worked up about something, somehow, and she ended up turning on Rudy and then got herself killed over this psychodrama shit."

"So what's going on with that?" Dennis asked. "Where are the Feds on this thing?"

"All I can say is they're either fucking idiots for not taking me on, or they're doing a pretty good job of acting like it. You know I'm not fucking crazy, you all know I'm aware and alert and that I know what I know. You know I wouldn't be telling you guys this shit if I didn't know what the hell I was talking about, and I sure as hell wouldn't be leaning this far forward in the foxhole if I didn't think there was something going on here, something that I have to do something about.

"I could just say fuck it and move on. DynCorp is hiring subcontractors, cutouts, for these quasi-black ops that no one wants to accept responsibility for - like the Pablo Escobar killing - the US didn't do this, but . . . we did. Like Che, the US

Drowning Creek

didn't kill him, but we 'facilitated' it." Leon paused for breath. "We've all known assholes who've worked both sides."

"Are you saying Rudy was working both sides against the middle?" Steve asked.

"No," Leon said simply, "Ivy was."

There was a serious quiet in the room.

"It's the only thing that makes sense," Leon said. "Ivy was into this thing up to her eyebrows. Ivy was a party girl, Ivy loved her nose candy, and somewhere along the line Ivy's stripper girlfriends introduced her to this cool Colombian guy who partied like it was 1999 and had plenty of pixie dust. So Ivy was cozying up to Gato, and he saw her as a handy bitch to have about, somebody to use as a cut out or a mule – in fact he must have been using her somewhere within his operation, to the tune of so much money that when Ivy sensed Rudy was becoming aware of what she was into, she went berserk and started to slice and dice him." Leon paused again. "It wouldn't have been the first time she'd have used a straight razor on a man, by the way, but that's a whole other story I'll tell you some other time." Leon took a sip of whiskey.

"Ivy was working it through Gato and the FARC - her Special Forces contacts had gotten her in, and she was working both sides against the middle. But Rudy wasn't wise enough to figure things out. Letting Ivy become aware that he knew something about her goings-on left his six exposed, which was unwise to say the least. Both of them were playing a deadly game, Ivy trying to work the "other side" and Rudy snooping around like a one-man Sneaky Pete and we saw where it got them both. Rudy would have been much better off if he'd simply dropped her like a bad habit. But no, not a chance.

Rudy loved Ivy. Rudy would have been lucky if he'd only ended up going to jail, and not dead."

"So what are you going to do about it?" Dennis asked.

"I'll tell you what I'm not NOT going to do about it," Leon replied. "I'm not going to wait six months for some government wonks to do a feasibility study to prove that what I think is going on is actually happening. I'm gambling that I'm right and I'm going to move on it. I'm not going to let a bunch of bureaucrats tie up the whole thing in red tape designed mostly to cover their own asses. I'm taking the initiative and the responsibility. If that means going around and over everyone's head, then that's what I have to do. Action!"

"Alright," Dennis said again, "So what ARE you going to do about it? What's your plan?"

"This is what I'm going to do about it." Leon put an ashtray in the middle of the table. "This is the stadium." He put five playing cards face down around the stadium. "These are the white vans."

The crew leaned in.

"I'm going to the Army-Navy game, gonna tool around the parking lots looking for white vans. I see a white van, I'm calling the cops, calling the Feds, calling the whole fucking world. And if I see any of those Iranian fuckers moving around I'm gonna take 'em down, hog tie their ass, call the cops and move on to the next guy."

"You know, the tactic with those improvised mortar systems is to fire them remotely, right?" Dennis stated. "You know that, right?"

"Yeah, I thought about that."

"So what are you going to do about that?"

"I don't know," Leon admitted. "I haven't thought that far into it. What really needs to happen is this thing needs to be turned off right when those vans start rolling out from the No-Name gas station. But I'm only one man, I'm not a one man Army."

"You thought about disabling the vans? Putting sugar in their gas tanks, or something?"

"Yeah, I thought of that. I also thought of sneaking into the No-Name gas station at night, substituting the mortars propellant for an inert substance. Of course, both plans have a flaw in them."

"What's that?" Dennis asked.

"Like, how do I get that close to the vans? Gato isn't stupid, he's got to have some kind of security laid out on his operation, especially twenty-four to forty-eight hours out from initiating. I mean, that's how we would do it. I don't think we can physically get onto the No-Name gas station – I think it's a fairly safe assumption that Gato and his crew have some kind of security, and I don't want to alert them, have them bolt or go to ground, only to start up operations again somewhere else. That's a risk I don't think we can take."

"Well, shit," Dennis exclaimed.

"Yeah," Leon agreed. "Maybe there's a better way."

"What?"

"I dunno. I was actually hoping one of you could think of something. That's why I'm here telling you all of this."

"What about shooting out their tires?" Charlie suggested. "A bit of stand-off, suppressed .22 from the wood line. Gato and crew come out ready to roll out on their Mission from God and every van's got four flat tires."

"That might actually work," Leon said. "But then what? They're still out there, they still have their vans. Worst case scenario they've got enough tires in the repair bays to swap out and roll out of there. Shooting out all their tires is not a complete enough solution. Anyhow, then Gato and crew would know somebody's on to their shit, and they disappear. Doesn't solve the problem. Makes it worse, if anything."

"How about a few rifle rounds into the engine blocks?" Steve suggested. "Or better yet, 12-gauge slug?"

"This would be more effective," Leon admitted. "But it's predicated on the notion that all the vans are all staged at the gas station, prior to rolling out. What if they take the vans home, night before the attack? And again - once they know somebody's on to them, they scatter like rabbits."

"You already showed us the pic," Charlie said, "Where they all live in that one place – the place Rudy thought was a party house where Ivy was hanging out, right?"

"That's right, but I can't keep an eye on the gas station and be watching them at the house at the same time AND be stalking their asses at the football game all at the same time," Leon said. "That's the fucking problem with this whole damn thing – there are so damn many moving parts and I can't be in two or more places at the same time."

"That's what you got your bros for, bro," Dennis said.

Leon looked at Dennis. "You guys willing to get in on this thing with me?"

Dennis looked at Charlie. Charlie looked at Steve. Steve looked at Dennis. Then they all looked at Leon.

"Hell yeah, we're in!" Steve exclaimed. "Hunting humans, chasing down bad guys is what we do, right?"

"Well I guess now we got some manpower," Leon said. "Better some than none. Four individuals, so we can have eyes on the house and the gas station, so we'll know where they are and when they start to roll."

"Right," Dennis said. "Be better if we could rustle up some more help, it'd be better if each team is at least a two-man team, because two is one, and one is none, right? But at least this way one we've got one guy for each quadrant outside of the stadium and we can wing it from there."

"Look," Leon said, "the basic concept of the operation is to keep federal law enforcement fully informed from the second we think they're going operational. Then, hopefully infuse a sense of urgency into their asses.

"It's like that old joke," Leon went on. "A guy hears somebody rummaging through his shed, so he calls the cops. The cops say they're too busy, they'll send somebody around in the morning. So while he's still on the phone, the guy fires off a few rounds, says 'Never mind, I just took care of it myself.' Next thing you know there's five cop cars out in front of his place, a helicopter hovering overhead with a search light, cops all over the place. No body, no sign of foul play. The cops say, 'I thought you said you took care of it yourself?' Guy says back, 'I thought you said you were too busy?'"

This produced some smiles and chuckling.

"Each of you guys shows up at the game. Bring a friend. Better yet, bring two or three friends. Go to your assigned sector, and when you see a white van with an Iranian or Gato in it, go up to it, pull the motherfucker out, overpower his ass, put him on the deck, zip tie his ass, then call the cops."

"That's it?"

"That's it."

"That simple?"

"You know the deal," Leon said. "It's the KISS principle. Keep it simple, stupid."

"There's something I'm thinking about, can't get out of my head," Charlie said.

"What's that?"

"These improvised mortar tube systems are designed to be launched remotely, via cell phone. So we put the jump on the driver and/or operator sitting opposite of him – how does this disable the system?"

"You've got a point," Leon acknowledged.

"What about the vehicle's fuse box?" Steve spoke up. "Take that out, you've just disabled power to everything."

"You'd have to get on it pretty damn fast," Leon said.

"Well, if we had the resources, we could figure out how to transmit a jamming frequency for the cellphone initiators," Dennis said.

"That takes a lot of resources," Leon said. "You ever try it?"

Drowning Creek

"Not really, no," Dennis said.

"To jam frequencies over an area like that would take a transmitter powered by a generator that'd be so big, it'd take a semi-trailer to haul it around," Leon said, "and it would be jamming everyone's cell signal frequencies, not just the bad guys. Jamming frequencies is an FCC violation – basically a federal felony - and it wouldn't take long to track down who's got a big, giant-ass transmitter parked out in the parking lot."

"You said there are possibly five vans," Steve said. "There are only four of us."

"Yes," Leon acknowledged, "in fact, there may even be six vans, because Gato is out there tooling around as well, but I've never been able to put my finger on a fifth or a sixth van. Either way, we'll need at least two more teams."

The guys all looked at each other. "Should be enough talent in the bar downstairs," Dennis said.

"That's what I figure," Leon said.

"This is Pineland," Steve pointed out. "Any one of us could stand up a platoon around here, or a company even, at the snap of our fingers."

"That's why I'm talking to you guys," Leon said. "Because as crazy as you are, I know you're dependable, and you can get the job done."

"Hell," said Charlie, "we could get a bunch of Q course trainees, like the troopies down in the holding company waiting for class dates or healing up from injuries. We tell them this is an exercise, part of their training in the Q course, and use them for manpower."

"You know," Leon said, "That's so stupid it might actually work."

"Hey!" said Charlie, "You know what they say: if it's stupid but it works, it ain't stupid!"

"Are we doing anything illegal here?" Dennis asked.

"I'm not a lawyer," Leon replied. "I'd say what we're up to right now could be considered some kind of conspiracy, and it'd be illegal or whatever if what we were planning to do was illegal. But once we start yanking bad guys out of vans full of homemade mortar systems pointed into the inside of the stadium, throwing them to the ground and hog tying their asses, I don't think the law is going to have a problem with what we're doing – especially considering I have kept them fully informed every inch of the way, and all the evidence that's been accumulated over the course of the investigation."

"How bad could a thing like this backfire?" Dennis asked.

"I thought about that" Leon replied. "I war gamed every contingency, and if you like we can war game it again. In fact, you can all tag along with me back up to the FBI offices in Raleigh and we'll go over the whole damn thing with the Bureau all over again, show them everything we've got all over again, and tell them either they do something about it or we're gonna do it for them. Either way, a bunch of white vans show up at the Army-Navy Game, I'm gonna do something about it.

"Look, there's nothing in this for me," Leon concluded. "This is about Rudy Haglin. As far as I'm concerned there was never a nicer guy ever shit between a pair of combat boots, but somehow he drew the short straw on this whole thing because that's the way the Universe works sometimes. Rudy didn't deserve the cut of the cards he ended up with, the only thing he ever did wrong was to marry Ivy."

"Let me see if I got this right, then," Steve said. "You need a team of guys to handle four, five, maybe six white vans? And the Army-Navy game is when?"

"This weekend."

"Wow. Doesn't give us much time," Steve said.

"You just said you could stand up a platoon at the snap of your fingers," Leon pointed out.

"Tell you what, I can rustle up some manpower for you. Everybody meet over at my place tomorrow evening. Bring everything you've got, Leon. Hell, put together a frikkin power point presentation, if you like. I'll have your manpower."

"You guys are with me in this shit, then?" Leon asked.

"Hell, yeah!" said Steve.

"This sounds like too much fun!" said Dennis.

Charlie held his glass up. "This is for Rudy."

"For Rudy," they all returned.

XXIV

"Okay," Leon said to Nancy. "I've think I've got the tripwire figured out."

"Tripwire?" Nancy asked.

"I want to ask something of you, and you don't have to do it if you don't want to."

"Is this something kinky?"

"Ha, ha. No, not this time," Leon said. "This is what I want to ask if you'll do. I want is for you to fly the drone over this No-Name gas station, off Highway One. There's a bunch of white vans I'm interested in," Leon said. "All I want you to do is park somewhere innocuous, launch the drones and keep an eye on the place, let me know when they roll out of there."

"Shouldn't we let the cops know about this? Maybe the FBI?"

"I told them," Leon answered. "I told them all about it. I told Army CID, and the FBI. I don't know what the hell these guys are up to but its like they're all sitting on their thumbs doing jack shit. All I'm asking you to do is go up there on Saturday, there's a part of the turn off that's got a wide shoulder where you can back it into the stand of pine trees and park. Fly the drone, keep an eye on the place, and when the vans roll out of there, let me know."

"Okay," Nancy said. "I'll do it. But you're going to owe me after this."

Drowning Creek

"I'll pay you," Leon said. "How much do you make on a Saturday night?"

"Two to three thousand. Sometimes as much as four."

"Can we go with two?" Leon asked.

"Okay," Nancy replied, "but you're still going to owe me."

"No problem. You got any problem with packing heat?"

"I'm okay with that," Nancy said matter-of-factly.

"Good. Let's go inside." He retrieved a pistol from his gun safe, handed it to Nancy. Her fingertips moved over its contours. A glint of recognition sparked in her eyes, catching him off guard. "Nice," she remarked, "CZ-75. Fine Czech craftsmanship, short recoil, locked-breech design, chambered in nine millimeter — accurate and versatile. One of my personal favorites."

"Not bad," Leon said. "You actually know guns." In his head he was saying, *'This girl just climbed up another rung on the ladder from squeeze to girlfriend to . . . this one could be a keeper . . .'*

Nancy dropped the magazine – it was empty - locked the slide to the rear, inspected the chamber, looked down into the magazine well, then looked at the chamber again. Then she released the slide catch and the slide snapped forward with a metallic snap.

"Impressive," Leon said, "You actually know how to lock and clear a weapon. You sure you didn't do any time in the infantry?"

Nancy smiled. "My Daddy was a Navy SEAL," she shrugged. "Got any nine mill?"

XXV

Steve's place was crowded, standing room only around a table he'd set up in his living room. "If you're here, you're in it," Steve said. "You're in it because we asked for help and every one of you guys said you're willing to help a brother. There's no money in it, there's no fame or glory. In fact if we fuck up there's gonna be a lot of infamy and notoriety and quite probably some legal fallout." Steve paused for effect. "It's not as if no one in this room hasn't ever walked down that road before. This is for our fallen brother Rudy Haglin, to clear his name and to possibly shut down some evil shit that's about to go down and this is why we called out to the brotherhood. If you don't want to be in it, leave now. There's the door."

Nobody moved.

"Good." Steve went on. "Leon has been working like a one-man National Strategic Asset to bring some light on this shit but nobody – not the Feds, not Army CID, or CI, nobody - is giving a shit and so Leon was prepared to do what he had to do singlehandedly, if necessary. I told him I'd get him some help and that's why y'all are here. I'll let Leon take it from here."

There was some murmuring around the table. "Hello everybody, and thanks for showing up. I'm humbled, I truly am," Leon began. "You have no idea the uphill battle I've been fighting trying to get some kind of traction on this thing." Leon went on to tell them the whole story, starting with fishing Ivy's body out of the creek, visiting Rudy in the brig, what he learned about Gato and his crew out at the No-Name gas station, and his encounters with CID and the Feds.

'This getting to be like Ground Hog Day,' Leon thought as he went through the entire thing all over again, showing slide shots of the pics he had laid out on the table the night before at the Irish pub.

"The plan is simple," he went on. "I've got a stake out in place on the white vans at the No-Name gas station. When the vans start rolling, we'll know they're enroute to the stadium."

Leon went on. "Gato and his crew show up at the stadium for the Army-Navy Game with their fleet of white vans, and we're waiting for them. The vans contain the mortar systems – the six white tubes I showed you. It's assumed they're electrically primed firing systems, actuated remotely via cell phone switch.

"We're expecting them. We lay in wait. When the white vans show up, walk up like you own the place, yank the asshole behind the wheel out onto the pavement and kick his ass, and pull all the van's fuses, disable all electrical power to the vehicle. To the best of my knowledge there are four vans but there might be five – in fact we may have to be prepare for as many as six - so we'll need at least one team in reserve, which is just good planning anyway."

A hand went up. "Yeah," Leon said.

"Pulling all the fuses is going to take a little time. Not much, but enough time for some asshole to send the signal to the cellphone to fire the tubes." It was a younger guy that Leon didn't know.

"Yes, this crossed my mind but it's the best I got," Leon admitted. "Why? What do you suggest?"

"Well, there's a couple of ways to go about this, and your way is one of them, but that's assuming they haven't wired their firing system to an independent power source. That's the way I'd do it. All you need is a couple of those six-volt lantern batteries, or a motorcycle battery, even."

"Yeah," Leon replied. "That actually crossed my mind, but I guess that's the course of action I was ignoring. I can't think of everything, and it does complicate things a bit. For example, what if it's more than a simple circuit wired in parallel? What if there's three wires coming off the battery? In other words, it's wired so that if you cut the wrong wire everything goes off anyway."

"Well, first of all," the young guy said, "why would anyone go to the trouble of wiring it that way for a firing system on what is basically improvised artillery? That would make sense if you were making some kind of booby trap, but doesn't make sense in this case. But regardless of how they wire the things, there's still the challenge of trying to physically disable it before it can be fired remotely, via cellphone."

"Right," Leon said. "You've identified the problem, what's your solution?"

"Why not jam the cellphone signal?"

"I think that's why I was ignoring it," Leon said. "Jamming is incredibly complex, especially over the area we're talking. We'd need a generator powered by at least a five thousand kilowatt generator to cover the entire surrounding environs of a football stadium, and even then we have no guarantee of effectiveness."

Drowning Creek

"Right," the young guy said. "But what about shutting down the cell towers? Then the cellphones won't be able to send and receive, because they're cellular, right?"

"Right," Leon said, "How do we do that? There are so many cell towers – they're on top of buildings, on the sides of water towers, everywhere, and there are so many providers. It would take a government level operation to get all the companies to cooperate to turn off their signals, and that's part of the problem – the government is ignoring me. After Rudy Haglin got his head blown off, they called it a suicide and closed the investigation."

"Oh yeah," the young guy said, "if you go the legal route. But this is the internet era." He pointed at Leon's laptop on the table. "We hack into the cell companies, find the towers we want to shut down – basically everything within twelve miles of the stadium – and we shut them down."

"See? This is why I needed help with this damn thing," Leon said, looking over at Steve. "A guy can't think of every fucking thing, especially a knuckle dragging Neanderthal like me. I can fight my way out of a saloon full of bikers – in fact I've done it - I can shoot a flea off the balls of a buffalo at fifty paces with iron sights, but I never would have thought about hacking into a cellphone network, never in a million years.

"Anyway, you look familiar, young man," Leon continued. "Where do I know you from?"

"You made a night jump with us, east of Mackall," the young man grinned. "Then you told us how to sneak past the 82d Airborne by doing it the SF way. You know – if you ain't cheatin', you ain't tryin'. . ."

"... and if you get caught, you ain't tryin' hard enough," everyone around the table repeated, like a mantra. They were all grinning like idiots.

"Oh yeah, right," Leon answered. "Glad to see you made it through the Q Course. Good to have you on the team. How do you know Steve?"

The young man looked over to Steve. "You want to tell him, Dad, or should I?"

Steve was grinning his evil grin from ear to ear. "H-e-e-e-y what can I say, Brother? Blood is thicker than water, right?"

"When Dad told me it was you, wild horses couldn't have dragged me off of this operation," the young man said.

"W-O-A-H-!-!-! Good to know," Leon said. "Glad I didn't fuck with you guys too hard. Just goes to show, you never know who you're dealing with.

"Moving on," Leon continued, "we need to rehearse the operation, we need to at least do a tabletop drill, then we're going to have to do a technical rehearsal on shutting down the cell towers – I want to see if your shit actually works – and then of course we're going to have to develop a commo plan. Our phones are obviously out of the picture because if the towers are down, then everyone's phone comm's are down. I'll get my hands on some radios." He unrolled a large sketch of the stadium where he'd outlined the perimeter of the stadium, parking lots, adjacent streets and other notable features. "But right now I want to war game this new angle to the plan, shutting down the cell towers." Leon looked at Steve's kid. "How can you guarantee this thing will work, if you're on your laptop, on the net, remotely, via a cell signal, and all the towers are shut down? I mean, that would mean your connectivity is gone as well, right?"

"Right," the young man answered. "but A) the damage is temporary, and B) . . ."

"Wait a minute" Leon interrupted. "What's your name, anyway? I keep wanting to call you Steve's kid, but . . ."

"Fred," the young man replied.

"Fred? Who calls their kid Fred???" Leon asked.

"I named him after Federico Fellini," Steve spoke up, "but we all call him Fred."

"Fair enough," Leon remarked. "Good name. Fellini made some great films. In fact, this thing is sizing up to be like one of them."

The meeting proceeded, into the detailed planning and war gaming phase.

"With the cell towers out, this simplifies things significantly," Leon said. "Now we don't have to worry about being able to physically disable the firing systems to the launchers – we've taken out the cellphone signal. Now all it comes down to is getting the drop on whichever asshole you're covering down on and beating his ass, taking out some stress on a deserving target.

"Best of all, it's not even illegal, not even in a shady gray area. I mean, the last time I checked it's not illegal to stop a terrorist attack that's in progress. Especially if we're doing it with just our bare hands."

"Kind of illegal to take out cellular networks," Fred remarked.

"Well, yeah, there's that," Leon replied. "What are the odds they can track it back to us?"

"Virtually zero. We can make it look like a Macedonian troll farm did it."

"A Macedonian troll farm!" Leon exclaimed. "I like that!"

XXVI

This was it, show time. In Chapel Hill the crowds had been arriving throughout the day, pulling tail gate parties and slowly filling the stadium, warming up with the pre-game activities.

The teams were staked out around the stadium, covering all four quadrants, parked at the edges of the parking lots looking towards the stadium. For two-way radio communications, Leon had equipped everyone with hand-held MURS* radios that provided short-distance, two-way voice or data communications transmitting across a narrow frequency band, and importantly, did not require a license. With a power limit of 2 watts, range operation was within 2-3 miles for a handheld unit, up to 10 miles for vehicle mounted units with an externally mounted antenna.

Leon's radio crackled – it was Nancy.

"The vans are rolling."

"Gotcha. Thanks."

Leon and the rest of the guys were positioned around the stadium. The support crew was manning a small fleet of drones hovering over key intersections, keeping their eyes out for white vans with distinctive canvas covered hatches on their roofs.

---

* Multi-Use Radio Service

Peter Crittenden

In the back seat of Leon's truck, Steve's son Fred was doing his thing on his laptop. Leon sent out a series of radios checks come over the walkie-talkie:

"Goat Roper this is Sugar Bear. Commo check, over."

"Sugar Bear this is Goat Roper, I read you Lima Charlie, how you me, over?" Loud and clear.

"Goat Roper this is Sugar Bear, I got you. Hog Slayer, this is Sugar Bear, commo check, over."

"Sugar Bear, this is Hog Slayer, I got you Lima Charlie."

"Hog Slayer this is Sugar Bear, good copy. Cool Breeze, this is Sugar Bear, commo check, over."

"Sugar Bear this is Cool Breeze. I read you, over."

"That's good copy Cool Breeze. Break, Hello Kitty this is Sugar Bear." He'd given Nancy a radio, just in case she needed to talk to him or if he needed to talk to her. "Radio check, over."

"Sugar Bear, this is Hello Kitty, I read you loud and clear, over."

"Rotor Head, this is Sugar Bear, radio check, over."

"Sugar Bear, this is Rotor Head. I read you Lima Charlie, over."

"Sand Pounder, this is Sugar Bear, radio check, over."

"Sugar Bear, this is Sand Pounder. Lima Charlie, over."

"Sex Machine, this is Sugar Bear. Come in, over."

"Sugar Bear, this is Sex Machine. Lima Charlie, over."

Drowning Creek

'Goat Roper, Hog Slayer, Cool Breeze, Hello Kitty, Rotor Head, Sand Pounder, Sex Machine,' Leon rolled his eyes. *'This is what you get when you let a bunch of Green Berets and a stripper choose their own codenames.'*

"Okay everybody, it's Prom Night – you all know what to do. You see a white van, check out the roof, see if it looks like it's got a cut out, fabric covered. Take a good hard look at the driver and if he's one of our guys, let him have it."

Now it was time to wait. To watch, and wait. Just like laying and waiting on an ambush. Leon kicked back and rubbed his eyes. Ever since he pulled Ivy out of Drowning Creek this entire affair had been an epic stress fest, all the meetings with CID, CI, the Feds, the whole thing with Rudy, getting shot at – so much happening in all directions with him in the middle of it all, it was amazing that he hadn't broken out in hives or something. But now it was do or die. Within the next hour they'd know if Gato's crew were going operational or if it really was all a pipe dream on his behalf. And if what Leon thought was going down actually was about to go down, he had his own private army in place and they were ready to do something about it.

Suddenly the radio started going off like it was Halloween meets the Fourth of July all at once - the white vans were rolling into the parking areas around the stadium all at the same time, apparently. "Show time," Leon said to Fred. "Do your thing."

Fred nodded and entered a command into the black screen full of code he was looking at, then he looked up at Leon. "Check your phone."

"Phone's dead in the water," Leon said.

"It's done," said Fred.

"That fast?" Leon asked.

"That fast."

"Good." No sooner had he said that, a white van rolled into the portion of the parking lot they were locked down on. Leon's eyes went hard when he realized it was Gato behind the wheel.

Leon picked up his walkie-talkie. "All Snake Eaters," he said in a sure, firm voice, "All Snake Eaters, this is Sugar Bear. I have eyes-on Shithead Number One. Going dynamic – do what you gotta do - EXECUTE! EXECUTE! EXECUTE!"

Leon was watching Gato's white van so hard he felt like he had laser beams emitting out of his eyeballs. When Gato cracked the driver's side door open, Leon made his move. He un-assed his truck, charged the white van and yanked the door open. Gato looked at Leon, startled and wild eyed. Leon grabbed Gato by the back of his collar and pulled him out of the van, all the way down to the ground. Leon put a knee on Gato's chest, pinning him to the pavement. Leon grabbed Gato around Gato's neck with his left hand and squeezed, hard.

Gato's hands instinctively went to Leon's left wrist in an attempt to break the choke hold, while Leon started pounding Gato's face with his free hand.

Gato squirmed under Leon's weight, grimacing at the punishment Leon was delivering. Leon became aware of Gato reaching down, he was going for a pistol tucked into the waistband of his trousers. Leon moved his left knee to secure Gato's wrist. Gato took the opportunity to reach up with his other hand and claw at Leon's eyes. Leon rolled to the left,

Drowning Creek

pinning Gato's gun hand beneath his body weight. Gato rocked hard side to side, built up some momentum and managed to roll up on top of Leon.

'*Shit.*'

Now Gato was on top, Leon was on his back, and each man now had a hand on the other's throat. Leon clenched the muscles in his neck - Gato's grip was having minimal effect, while Leon's large hand on Gato's scrawny neck was squeezing the life out of the smaller man. Gato's eyes were starting to bulge out.

Meanwhile Leon rolled his bodyweight over Gato's right wrist, grinding Gato's scrawny wrist between his hip and the pavement. Leon heard a sound like bones being crushed. Gato grimaced in pain and finally let go his grip on Leon's throat. The wiry Gato did an arm sweep to break Leon's grip off his throat and attempted another gouge at Leon's eyes which caused Leon to flinch and instinctively block with his free hand. This gave Gato a chance to roll off.

Gato scrambled to his feet and stood over Leon. His injured right hand hanging uselessly by his side, Gato was attempting to draw the pistol on his right hip with his left hand. Leon somehow came up into a crouch and exploded like a panther, knocking Gato down again. Leon was on top this time, pinning both of Gato's arms. He began again with the punishing open-handed slaps while reaching down behind his left leg in an attempt to secure Gato's pistol. The wiry smaller man thrashed about with the strength and power of a cornered animal as both men struggled in what was obviously a fight to the death.

Peter Crittenden

Somehow Gato wriggled free and scampered away, running past the white van to a nearby row of parked cars. Breathing hard and hurting all over, Leon struggled to his feet. He watched Gato opening the door on a blue Dodge Challenger.

'FUCK. A Dodge Challenger, a blue Dodge Challenger!' Leon's mind was racing. Where had he seen that before? Leon knew he'd seen it before, but in the rush of adrenaline pumping through his veins, all he could think of was the task at hand:

'Get Gato.'

Leon ran back to his truck. He couldn't let Gato get away now. "Get over into your car!" he hollered at Fred, "Get on the horn, and tell everybody I'm chasing fuckin' Gato, he's in a fuckin' blue Dodge Challenger!"

"What do I do? What do I do?" Fred asked.

"You're in charge!" Leon hollered back. "Take charge!"

Fred bailed out the passenger side of the van, his laptop tucked under his arm. Leon was popping the parking brake and dropping the van into gear when there was a fast series of loud knocks on his driver's side window. It was Kleckner, one of the FBI guys. Leon opened the window. Kleckner reached in and put his hand on Leon's shoulder. "Stop, Leon!" he ordered. "You're interfering with a federal investigation!"

"You guys didn't tell me you were gonna be here! You didn't tell me anything!"

"Need to know, Leon!" Kleckner responded. "You didn't need to know!"

Drowning Creek

"The hell you say!" Leon shouted as he hit the accelerator and roared away. He was going after Gato. The Challenger was already at the exit of the parking lot, but Leon was right on his tail. Leon raced through town as fast as he could to make the traffic lights behind Gato. When they got to the turnoff to the highway Leon gunned his truck. The big block sucked in air through its valves, burning diesel like jet fuel as the cylinders rattled to 2800 rpms and 380 horsepower surged the truck forward. Gato had the edge in the Challenger but Leon had a pretty good idea where he was going - one of two places – the No-Name Gas Station, or back to his crib. All Leon had to do was tail him.

When Gato took the off-ramp to the No-Name, Leon was on him. He pulled into the gas station right behind him. Gato got out of the van and moved towards the gas station's office. Leon un-assed his truck and ran right at Gato.

Leon ran around the blue Challenger to where Gato was fumbling with his keys on the front door of the shop. Gato turned and looked at him, eyes wide, and turned to run to the alley between the office and the work bays. Leon slammed into him like a linebacker and both men went to the concrete. As Leon struggled to get on top, Gato reached out and grasped a piece of iron rebar, bringing it down in a glancing blow across the side of Leon's head. It hurt like hell but it wasn't a direct blow. Momentarily dazed, Leon struggled to maintain some kind of control over the smaller man, who was scrambling backwards like a crab on a beach.

The area between the two buildings was littered with garbage cans, plastic milk crates, old cardboard boxes and miscellaneous debris. Free from Leon, Gato overturned a garbage can before turning to flee. This bought Leon precious seconds to close on Gato, get his hands on him as they both careened off the walls of the narrow alley. Gato clawed at Leon's eyes but Leon's longer arms were able to hold him off just enough. Still, the Latin's fingernails scraped at Leon's face. Leon managed to get his hands around Gato's throat and started to squeeze.

Gato's eyes swelled and the veins in his neck bulged. The struggle went into a kind of a dance as Leon moved about to avoid Gato's attempts to knee him in the groin. Then Leon felt something sharp grazing his side and looking down he saw a screwdriver in Gato's fist. Gato managed to jam the screwdriver into Leon's side. The pain was unbelievable – white hot - and Leon's grasp around Gato's throat weakened. The smaller man flailed at Leon, cutting his face with the bloody screwdriver. Leon slammed his fist into Gato's face, but his side wound was already sapping his strength and the wiry South American was able to withstand the blow, even wiggle out of Leon's grasp.

The stab wound must have been worse than Leon initially thought, his strength was failing fast. Breathing hard, Leon felt his surroundings starting to spin. He saw a puddle of blood on the pavement in front of him and he knew the blood was his. Leon's legs went weak, his knees buckled and he went down.

Glancing up, Leon saw Gato backing away and looking about for another weapon. Gato tossed the screwdriver aside and picked up a piece of wood - a two-by-two inch by about four foot long piece of wood with a nail sticking out of it. Gato swung this chunk of wood like he was warming up with a baseball bat. Brandishing his new weapon, Gato moved towards Leon. Leon tried to scramble away but seemed almost unable to move, his arms and legs felt like they were filled with lead.

Drowning Creek

Gato stood over Leon, holding his weapon aloft. All Leon could do was brace himself for the coming blow as he desperately looked about for something, anything to shield himself or fight back with. His heartbeat was pounding in his head like a drum, he was dizzy and everything was spinning around him. Leon knew he was losing it. Looking up at Gato, Leon felt like this was it. *'This is gonna suck,'* he thought as he grimaced in anticipation of what was to come next.

The phenomenon of seeing one's life flash in front of one's eyes is real. Waiting for the fatal blow, Leon saw a complex series of images flash before his eyes, in his mind's eye he saw many, many things – childhood memories he'd long forgotten, friends that he hadn't seen in years, decades, his mother even, long since passed on. It was like a stop-frame movie was flickering on the inside of his skull - every scene, every moment happy and sad, everything he had ever done, said, experienced. It was like time itself was spread out in a kind of panorama where the past, the present and even the yet-to-be future co-existed, simultaneously.

And then he was back in the horrible reality from which there was no escape. Leon was flat on his back, crushed, defeated, unable to move as Gato paused for a split second before he brought down the cudgel.

There was a crashing roar of sound but no feeling of blows or pain. Leon looked up, startled to see Gato's face turn from a grimace of hate to a look of stunned surprise as blood spurted from two holes in the center of his chest. Gato dropped the stick and clutched at himself. Then another roar of sound and a red dot appeared in Gato's face - right between the eyes - and the back of his head blew out behind him. The thin man crumpled to the ground.

Leon turned his head back and saw Nancy standing behind him, legs apart in a classic shooters stance. Smoke was curling out of the barrel of the slab-sided CZ-75 she was holding in both hands, muzzle pointing down. "Thank God," Leon croaked. Then, "Where the hell did you learn to shoot like that?"

"I told you," Nancy said, "my Daddy was a Navy SEAL."

* * *

Leon pulled himself up off the ground and moved towards Gato's crumpled body. Nancy came up and watched as Leon rifled through Gato's clothing. There was a wallet with a thick wad of one hundreds – Leon took the cash, left the ID and credit cards and stuffed the wallet back in Gato's pocket. He helped himself to Gato's watch.

"You always rob your dead?" Nancy asked.

"Sure, why not?" Leon shrugged. "He doesn't need it anymore."

Then Leon noticed a small, silver chain around Gato's neck. Something was weighing it down, around the side of his neck, behind his shoulder. Leon pulled it up – it was a cogwheel, of an unusual alloy. An alloy that Leon had seen before, a cogwheel exactly like the wheels in the device.

The Fifth Wheel.

Leon yanked the chain off Gato's dead neck, looked back at Nancy. "Let's get the hell out of here."

Epilogue

Leon and Nancy rolled down the highway in his truck.

"That was close, Leon," Nancy said. "That was damn close."

"Thank you for being there."

"I'm glad I was."

The chatter on the radio had subsided – the teams had intercepted their targets, the white vans, just in time. The Feds had been all over that place as well and the guys did what Green Berets do – got the hell out of Dodge, dodged the bullet and let somebody else take the blame or the credit for the mess they'd left behind.

"I've got some water in a bottle in my rucksack, in the back there," Leon said. "Can you get it for me, please?"

Nancy reached back, rummaged through the bag and pulled out a steel flask. "You'd better pull over so we can clean you up a bit, before we pull into a gas station or something. You're a mess."

"Thanks," said Leon. He pulled a large green rag out of a cargo pocket on his trousers. "Here, can you put some water on this?" He started wiping his face and hands.

A rest area came up and they pulled over, parked in a shady area beneath a large chestnut tree and got out. Nancy helped Leon clean up. "There's some soap in my ruck," Leon said, "and my crash kit, a trauma first aid kit."

"Holy Hell, you're a mess," Nancy said.

"You should see the other guy," Leon quipped. To that, Nancy remained silent as she went about daubing his bloodied face. "We gotta look at what he did to me with the screwdriver," Leon said. He grimaced as he pulled off his shirt.

Nancy's eyes went wide as she inspected the wound. "Oh my God."

"What is it?" Leon asked, "Is it bad?"

"It's a nasty gash, Leon. A lot of blood."

"Is it a puncture wound?"

"Sort of. It sort of goes into the meat. It looks real nasty. Looks like it really hurts."

"It hurts like hell," Leon grunted. "I'm hopin' it isn't deep. What kind of blood do you see?"

"Dark," Nancy said. "Sort of oozing out of there, almost like jelly. Thick, dark blood."

"Good," Leon said. "I don't think it punctured the lung. If it did, the blood would be bright red and frothy, full of bubbles, and I'd be feeling it worse than I do, drawing a deep breath."

"We need to get you to a doctor, Leon. This is bad."

"Clean it up, put on some of that antibiotic ointment, and patch it," Leon replied. "I'll go see one of the team medics for sutures and a tetanus shot. Don't need to be answering any stupid questions about any kind of fight went down last night."

While Nancy worked on his side, Leon fumbled around his shirt lying in his lap. He reached into the breast pocket and withdrew the cogwheel on its broken chain, the cogwheel he'd retrieved off Gato's body. "Hey," he said to Nancy, "Remember this thing?"

"Oh yeah," she replied.

"Can you pull the rucksack over here, please?" Leon reached inside his rucksack and pulled out the device. He popped open the hatch on the device and looked at the four wheels, and the open space for the fifth. They both looked at it, at the wheel in Leon's hand, then at each other.

"Can we get internet out here?" Leon asked.

"I think so," Nancy replied. "We're outside the footprint Fred used to wipe out the towers. We oughta be able to use a phone as a hotspot."

"Can we be tracked?"

"Well, that depends on what you mean 'tracked'," Nancy answered. "Yes, it's possible. But it's also possible to make it look like – for anyone trying to figure out who we are - that we're . . ."

". . . a Macedonian troll farm?"

"Yes, if that's what you want. Or anything, anywhere, really."

"Okay," Leon said. He pulled his laptop out of his ruck, put it on the console between him and Nancy. "This thing," he said, handing her the device. "The crypto thing," he said, indicating the laptop with his chin. "Bring it up."

Nancy got to work establishing a blind connection, then going into the bowels of the internet. Leon handed her the little cogwheel, the fifth wheel. "Here you go. Put it in. Open this thing up, and tell me what we've got."

Nancy dropped the cogwheel into its space, in line with the four other cogwheels in the device. The device whirred, a series of digits scrolled upon the liquid crystal display. Nancy's eyes widened at what she saw upon the screen. "Oh my God," she gasped.

"Whaddya got, Nancy?"

"Oh my God," she gasped again, her voice dropping to a whisper. "Oh my God . . . oh my God . . ."

Leon glanced over to the screen. He saw double digit numbers with nine sets of zeroes behind them.

Billions. Hundreds of billions. Billions of billions.

"Does this mean what I think it means?" he asked.

Nancy looked like she was going apoplectic, almost as if she was having a sort of silent epileptic fit. "Oh Leon," she gasped. "Leon . . . that's a lot of money!"

"That sure looks like a lot of money, but what does it mean? Can we get our hands on that money?"

"Leon," Nancy said quietly. "You have access to this crypto account, and you can do anything you want with it. In fact, you can do anything you want to do, anything in the world. Basically, Leon, you're rich."

"No, Honey - WE are rich," Leon stated simply. Nancy looked at him, didn't say a word. "I couldn't have done it without you. In fact," Leon continued, "if it wasn't for you, I'd be dead."

Leon pulled a fresh t-shirt and a sweatshirt out of the rucksack and enduring a bit of discomfort from the wound on his side, he pulled them on. He glanced about at the cars and trucks coming into the rest area from the highway, and the

Drowning Creek

comings and goings of the people. "Let's get back on the road," he said. "We need to keep moving."

They drove for awhile in silence as they both contemplated the information revealed by the device. After awhile Leon asked, "How rich are we, Honey?"

"Richer than all the billionaires in the world," Nancy said simply.

Leon concentrated on driving while trying to ignore his pain. He finally spoke, "Are you shitting me?"

"I shit you not."

Leon was silent for awhile, focusing on the road while he digested what Nancy had just told him. "Well, this thing ain't over yet," he said. "There's still one final detail needs attending to before we're home free."

"What's that?" Nancy asked.

Leon pulled off Highway 1 onto the little road that was the back way into Camp Mackall. "Someplace we gotta go," he said simply. "Something we gotta do."

They crossed over the bridge that went over the railroad tracks and drove past the main compound of the Camp Mackall training complex. Leon turned south, then east at the entrance, towards Fort Bragg. About three quarters of a mile down the road they came to the double bridges. Leon pulled the tuck over to the shoulder.

Nancy looked puzzled. "Give me the gun," Leon said. Nancy withdrew the pistol from its holster, dropped the magazine, pulled the slide back, cleared the round out of the chamber and handed it to Leon. Leon nodded, appreciatively.

Peter Crittenden

Leon held the pistol in two hands, depressed the takedown and removed the slide from the lower frame. He took out the recoil spring and follower and removed the barrel. He opened the driver side door and got out of the truck.

"What are you doing, honey?" Nancy asked.

"Saying goodbye to a friend," he replied.

Leon walked around the front of the truck to the bridge railing and tossed the barrel of the gun way out into the swamp. The piece of metal made a little bloop sound as it hit the water. Then he walked over to the other side of the bridge and threw the slide out there. Another bloop. Then he threw the frame. Bigger bloop.

Leon looked at the black waters of Drowning Creek for a few moments. It was over. His whole theory had been correct, he'd been right all along, right from the start, all about Gato and his crew. Now Gato, Haglin and Ivy were dead. Gato needed killing. With Haglin it was a damn shame. As for Ivy, well she had some bad karma that finally caught up with her.

It was over.

Leon got back into the truck, put her in gear and they proceeded down the road. The sun was shining, the air was fresh, and it was a beautiful day.

He was rich, richer than all the billionaires in the world . . . rolling down the road with his girl by his side, right now this was the best place to be in the entire world . . .

. . . and it was a beautiful day.

www.blacksmithpublishing.com